"Do you always do what the elders say?" Both Ethan and Charity quoted rules and words of others. Did they ever think for themselves?

"*Gelassenheit,*" he said. "That's German for patience and resignation. It means obedience to the Amish community. It is not something we *do*. It is something we *are*."

Leah had been raised to be on her own. Her mother's many marriages, their frequent moves and different schools had taught her to be independent. But she saw quite clearly that for the Amish, individuality was not a virtue. It was a curse. She stood. "Well, it looks like we've come full circle, Ethan. You were right after all—the English and the Amish can't mingle."

He stood too. "But we can care about one another," he said carefully. "We can always care."

She knew he meant *care* in a brotherly way. But after spending time with him, she didn't want to be just another sister to him. She wanted to be a girl who mattered to him the way Martha Dewberry mattered. Except that Leah wasn't Amish. And she never would be.

ANGELS
WATCHING
OVER ME

Lurlene McDaniel

ANGELS WATCHING OVER ME

BANTAM BOOKS

NEW YORK • TORONTO • LONDON • SYDNEY • AUCKLAND

RL 4.7, AGES 012 AND UP

ANGELS WATCHING OVER ME
A Bantam Book / November 1996

The Starfire logo is a registered trademark of Bantam Books, a division of Bantam Doubleday Dell Publishing Group, Inc. Registered in U.S. Patent and Trademark Office and elsewhere.

ISBN 0-553-56724-1

Published simultaneously in the United States and Canada

Bantam Books are published by Bantam Books, a division of Bantam Doubleday Dell Publishing Group, Inc. Its trademark, consisting of the words "Bantam Books" and the portrayal of a rooster, is Registered in U.S. Patent and Trademark Office and in other countries. Marca Registrada. Bantam Books, 1540 Broadway, New York, New York 10036.

PRINTED IN THE UNITED STATES OF AMERICA
OPM   10 9 8 7 6 5 4 3 2 1

*This book is dedicated to the memory of
Emily Anne Thomas, a loyal reader
and a precious child of God.*

"Are not all angels ministering spirits sent to serve those who will inherit salvation?" (Hebrews 13:2, New International Version)

ONE

"Well, I can't believe a broken finger can land you in the hospital, Leah. Are you telling me everything? Are you sure those doctors know what they're doing? I expected Indiana to be a little more progressive. Even if we are living in the boondocks."

Leah Lewis-Hall gripped the phone receiver. Her mother sounded as if she were next door instead of halfway around the world in Japan on her honeymoon. Leah took a deep breath, not wanting to scream at her mother. But she didn't want to let her know how scared she was either. *I'm sixteen and perfectly capable of handling the unexpected on my own,* she told herself. After all, nothing about her and her mother's lives together had ever approached what was expected all these years.

Patiently Leah explained, "I saw the doctor Neil said to call in case of an emergency. He did some X rays and blood work and told me my finger was broken. Then he told me I should come to the hospital and be checked out more thoroughly. So I did."

"How did you break your finger?"

"I don't know. After I took you and Neil to the airport, it just started hurting. I didn't bang it or anything. But it hurt so bad I couldn't even sleep last night." She didn't add that sleeping alone in the old farmhouse Neil was renovating for the three of them to live in wasn't exactly restful. "Maybe the doctor thought I should be in the hospital because the two of you are so far away."

"I want to talk to a doctor. Is one around?"

"Not right now. Neil's doctor said to call him at his office and he'd discuss it with you." Leah hated acting as go-between. What other girl her age had to check herself into the hospital alone?

Neil Dutton got on the phone. "What's going on, sugar?"

Leah wanted to shout, *"I'm not your sugar*

and you aren't my father!" Instead she explained the situation all over again.

Neil said, "Dr. Howser's a good man, and if he thinks you're better off in the hospital, then you are. Don't you worry, I'll call him and get the whole story and call you back later tonight. It's six A.M. here," he mused, "so that makes it—what? About four in the afternoon over there?"

"That's right." In Japan it was also a day later.

"I know we're a long way off, but if you want us to come home, we can be there in less than twenty-four hours."

Although being in the hospital frightened her, Leah certainly didn't want to interrupt her mother's new life. And she was positive that wasn't what her mother wanted either. Also, she vaguely remembered that Neil, a retired auto executive, had an important meeting scheduled with some Japanese businessmen on behalf of his former company. She said, "Please put my mother back on."

"Is that what you want us to do?" Roberta Dutton sounded cautious. "I mean, if you *want* us to come home—"

"No way," Leah interrupted quickly. "It's your honeymoon and I'm not a baby."

"Well, maybe we shouldn't act too hastily." Leah could almost hear the relief in her mother's voice. "I mean, wait until Neil talks to the doctor. Then we can decide what to do." She paused. "Japan's wonderful. I've already bought you some gorgeous things for Christmas, Leah. Why, I'll bet no girl in that new high school of yours will have anything as nice. I'm talking designer labels, no imitations." Her mother giggled. "Neil is positively pampering me."

Leah hated her mother's helpless-little-girl routine. Leah knew firsthand just how strong and *un*helpless her mother could be when it suited her.

"I'm sure I'll like whatever you've picked out," Leah said dutifully. It was Thursday, and Christmas was only nine days away. Since she was in the hospital, Leah was missing a few days of school, but so what? She really didn't have any friends at the high school yet. Maybe she *was* better off in the hospital.

Rural Indiana was a far cry from Dallas. Leah hated the cold weather, the dreary gray skies, the farm-country high school, the whole bucolic scene. She missed her friends and the sophistication of Dallas. So far, everybody she'd met seemed hopelessly hick and uncool. At least the hospital was in Indianapolis, a decent-sized city. Maybe she could persuade her mother to send her to a city high school starting in January. She could commute to the farm on weekends.

"So," her mother said, "it's settled. We'll talk to the doctor and call you later."

"Sure," Leah said listlessly. "No use rushing back until we know something more."

"That's my girl," Roberta said with a soothing lilt. "You were always so mature for your age, Leah. I know you can handle a few days in the hospital without me. While you're there, you get anything you want. Neil said he'd pay for it. Besides, I'm convinced that the doctor is overreacting. You're going to be perfectly fine, dear. Perfectly fine."

Leah hung up and scrunched down under the covers, hot tears brimming in her eyes.

A woman knocked on the door, and Leah quickly swiped her hand across her eyes. "Come in."

"Hi, I'm Molly Thasher, your day nurse. Just

call me Molly. I'm here to take temp and blood pressure. It's routine."

Molly's smile was so genuinely pleasant that Leah felt her spirits lift. "You don't look like a nurse," she told the thirty-something woman, whose long light-brown hair was clipped back by a gold barrette. She wore taupe slacks and a cranberry-colored long-sleeved shirt. A colorful Christmas pin on her shoulder twinkled with tiny lights.

"We try to dress real casual on the pedi floor. It's less scary for the younger kids."

"The pedi floor?"

"Pediatrics. You're in the adolescent area, but we're so crowded right now we may have to stack new patients in the hallway. I can't remember the pedi floor ever being this full." She slipped the blood pressure cuff around Leah's arm.

"Will I get a roommate?"

"You might. Each room can accommodate two patients, but it is possible to get a private room. Would you mind sharing?"

Leah thought about it and decided it didn't matter. Maybe she'd feel less isolated if she had a roommate. "Only if he's really cute," she told Molly.

The nurse laughed. "'Fraid not. Your roomie would definitely be female." Molly picked up Leah's left hand. Leah's forefinger had been strapped to a curved metal splint with gauze and tape.

Leah was embarrassed because her injury looked so insignificant. "My doctor isn't sure what's wrong with me."

Molly grinned. "Well, at least you're mobile. You should explore the place. We've got a nice game and rec room. Plenty of free snacks too, so long as you're not on a restricted diet. In fact, we're putting up a Christmas tree Saturday night; why don't you come help decorate it?"

Leah couldn't think of anything she'd like to do less. "I'll think about it," she said.

"So where are you from?" Molly pumped up the blood pressure cuff, and Leah felt it tighten around her arm.

Leah started to say "Dallas," but realized that Texas wasn't home anymore. "From Knightstown. My mother just remarried and the guy, Neil, bought this big farm and is fixing it up for us."

"Sounds exciting. That's pretty farm country."

It isn't to me, Leah thought, but she didn't say it. "Neil's always wanted to be a farmer. His first wife died a couple of years ago. He met Mom in Dallas three months ago and they just got married and went to Japan for their honeymoon." She wasn't sure why she was babbling on and on to Molly about things the woman probably couldn't care less about.

"My father was a career navy man, and he was once stationed in Japan," Molly said. "The country sounded so exotic to me, so romantic. Boy, did I ever want to go over and visit him."

"Didn't you get to?"

"No, he was back home in a year and then he got out of the service. He and my mother are retired now, and they have a condo here in Indy."

Leah had never known her father and never would. He'd left her and her mother when Leah was barely three, and he'd died when Leah was ten. In fact, aside from her mother, Leah didn't have any family. The only grandparent she'd ever known had been her father's mother, Grandma Hall, who had died from liver cancer when Leah was ten. And since Grandma Hall and Leah's mother didn't get along, it had been difficult for Leah to be a part of her grandmother's life.

Molly folded the blood pressure cuff. "I've lived all my life in Indiana, but I've always wanted to travel the world."

"Why don't you?" Leah couldn't imagine being stuck in one place all her life. Maybe because she and her mother had always moved around so much.

"Oh, I'm married, I have two kids, and we're settled. Maybe my husband and I will travel when we both retire."

It all sounded deathly boring to Leah. Molly started to leave. "Will you be back?" Leah asked, not wanting to be left alone.

"My shift ends soon, but the night shift is a great bunch of nurses. You'll like them." Molly paused at the doorway. "I'll see you tomorrow."

Leah offered a smile, but when she was alone she lay in the bed feeling sorry for herself. Sick of moping around, she decided to do some exploring. She climbed out of bed and felt her leg buckle as pain shot through her kneecap.

TWO

Leah grimaced and leaned against the bed, waiting for the throbbing to subside. *Now what's wrong?* The pain had an eerily familiar quality. Was her knee broken too? She took a deep breath and counted to ten. Gingerly she put weight on her leg, and thankfully her knee didn't give. She rubbed it. The knee was sore, but the sharp pain had gone away.

"Probably twisted it getting out of bed," she mumbled. She found her robe and went out into the hall.

The ward was a cheerful-looking place, with a spotless expanse of patterned linoleum that looked as if it belonged in a kitchen, not a hospital. The doors of the rooms were different bright colors, with animals painted across them and along the walls. A small sign on the wall marked one of the doorways as Toddler Ward 1. Farther down the hall, another door was painted to look like the open mouth of a rabbit. Its sign read Baby Ward.

Leah soon discovered that the entire floor was constructed like a giant wheel, with spoke-like halls leading to patient wards and rooms. At the hub of the wheel stood the nurses' station, a large circular desk where the nurses congregated, keeping track of charts and monitoring individual patients with computer screens and banks of machines. The younger and sicker patients were closest to the hub.

The long corridor walls were painted with scenes from fairy tales. There were two waiting rooms on the floor for parents and relatives. And in a spacious rec room Leah discovered a gathering of younger kids watching a *Snow White* video on a giant-screen TV. The rec room also had neon-colored plastic climbing toys, and the carpet was patterned with games such as hopscotch and tic-tac-toe.

Leah tried the three doors at the end of the room and discovered video games, a snack bar and kitchen, and a library. The snack bar's counter held bowls of fresh fruit, graham crackers and granola bars, and containers of fruit juices in bowls of ice. Vending machines lined one wall, and several tables stood in the center of the room. A young mother, patiently feeding a gaunt little boy, nodded at Leah. The boy had no hair and was attached to an IV line that led to a pole beside the table.

Leah shuddered. The little boy reminded her of Grandma Hall. Leah could remember visiting her sick grandmother in the hospital as though it were yesterday. Just like the little boy, her grandmother had been attached to an IV line and had been bald from chemotherapy treatments. At the time, her grandmother's wasted body had terrified Leah, who loved her grandmother dearly in spite of her mother's hostility.

Leah grabbed an apple from a bowl and retreated to the library, where she sorted through teen magazines in an attempt to forget the painful memories. She flopped onto a comfortable love seat and began to read. The magazines were filled with ideas for Christmas gifts and holiday fashions and only gave her pangs of homesickness.

All her friends, she was sure, would be going

to holiday parties and on shopping expeditions and skating at the ice rink at Dallas's Galleria Mall. She was stuck in a hospital while her mother was thousands of miles away. *No use feeling sorry for yourself,* Leah insisted silently. A glance at the clock showed that it was six.

Hoping she hadn't missed the dinner cart, Leah returned to her room but stopped just outside the doorway. Another bed had been placed in the room, and on it sat a girl who looked about five years old. The girl was sobbing and clinging to a woman dressed in a peculiarly old-fashioned style of clothing. Her dark blue skirt brushed the floor. The sleeves of her blouse were long, the neck high. A filmy white cap covered the woman's long hair, which was twisted into a bun at the nape of her neck. She wore no makeup and no jewelry, and she had no wedding band.

"There, there," the woman cooed soothingly. "Do not cry so, Rebekah. You're hurting my heart with such a flood of tears. You know I must go home to nurse the baby. But Charity and Ethan will come tomorrow."

"Don't go, Mama," the girl sobbed.

Feeling like an intruder, Leah wasn't sure what to do. Just then a man stepped from behind the open closet door. He too was dressed in a strangely old-fashioned way. His suit was dark, without lapels or buttons, and he held a broad-brimmed black hat in his big, rough hands. He had a beard but no mustache, and his long hair brushed the top of his collar. "Come, Tillie, the van's waiting downstairs. We've a long way to go tonight and it's beginning to snow."

"Papa," the child wailed, reaching for him. "Don't leave me, Papa." He hugged her tightly.

For the first time, the woman noticed Leah. "We did not mean to disturb you. Rebekah's scared, but she'll quiet down after we've gone."

Leah stammered, "I-It's okay. I don't mind. You're not bothering me one bit." Fascinated, she stared at the threesome. She stepped forward and held out her hand to the girl. "I'm Leah. We're going to be roommates."

The small girl's body quivered as she struggled to stop crying. "Leah?" she repeated, staring at Leah's flowered robe and dark, shoulder-length hair. "Are you a plain person?"

The question thoroughly confused Leah. "Plain enough."

"We're Jacob and Tillie Longacre," the girl's mother explained. "We're Amish."

Visions of photos Leah had seen of horse-drawn buggies and farms in Pennsylvania flashed in her head. She knew absolutely nothing about the Amish. She managed a cautious smile. "I—um—I'm just a regular person."

"We hate to leave our Rebekah, but we can't stay this night with her. Her sister Charity and her brother Ethan will come tomorrow, but until then she must be alone," Jacob explained.

"She's so young," Rebekah's mother said, wringing her hands.

"I'm not going anywhere," Leah said, feeling a surge of sympathy for little Rebekah. She knew what it felt like to be deserted. "Can we be friends?"

The girl was quiet. She bit her lower lip, picked up a rag doll and hugged it tightly against her chest. "Will you stay in the room with me?"

"That's my bed right there," Leah said, pointing across the room.

After a few more hugs and whispers, Rebekah's parents edged toward the door. At the doorway Tillie turned to Rebekah and said, "Remember what I've told you. The Lord's angel will watch over you until we can be with you." She smiled at Leah and said, "Thank you." And then they were gone.

For a moment Rebekah stared with wide blue eyes at the empty doorway. Slowly tears began to slide down her cheeks. Flustered, Leah reached out and awkwardly patted the tiny girl. "Would you like to watch TV?"

Rebekah shook her head.

"That's a pretty doll. What's her name?"

"Rose," Rebekah said, sniffing.

The doll was as unadorned as the child who clutched her. Rebekah wore a simple long nightdress with a high neck, and a cap like her mother's over a head of wispy golden curls. Her cheeks looked rosy, her blue eyes red and swollen from crying. Leah felt at a loss. She didn't have any siblings.

Rebekah looked up at her. "Are you an angel?"

"No way," Leah said with a smile. She sat on the edge of Rebekah's bed. "Do you know why you're in the hospital?"

Rebekah held out her arm. A bright red splotch stained the inside of her wrist and lower arm. It looked swollen. "A spider bit me. And I got sick."

Sitting close to the child, Leah could feel

heat emanating from her small body, and she realized that Rebekah's cheeks were rosy because of a fever. "Did you bite him back?" she asked.

Rebekah looked startled, then giggled. "No."

Making Rebekah laugh made Leah feel better than she had all day.

Two nurses bustled into the room, and Rebekah shrank back. "We have to put in an IV," one of the nurses explained.

Terrified, Rebekah shook her head.

"I'll stay with you," Leah said quickly.

One of the nurses eyed her. "Are you her sister?"

"Her roommate."

Rebekah clutched at Leah's hand. "Don't leave, Leah."

The single plea cut like a knife through Leah's heart, and she knew there was no way she could leave Rebekah.

Leah moved closer to Rebekah and reached for her small hand. "Look at me, not them," she instructed.

Obediently Rebekah fixed her gaze on Leah. "This is nothing," Leah said, hoping she sounded more convincing than she felt. "A piece of cake."

"Cake? Can I have some cake?"

Leah remembered the snack bar. "If it's all right with the nurse, I'll get you a cookie or something as soon as they're finished."

The nurse flipped open Rebekah's chart. "No food restrictions. The dinner cart's on its way, but a cookie would be fine."

"Lie still, honey," the technician said. "This will just be a little prick."

Leah smiled reassuringly at Rebekah, who lay rigid on the bed. From the corner of her eye, Leah watched the lab technician gently slide the needle of the IV under the skin on the back of Rebekah's hand. The child trembled, but she didn't move. Leah felt queasy. She watched as a tear slid from the corner of Rebekah's eye. "You're doing great," Leah said, still clasping Rebekah's hand.

Soon the IV was in and running, the tubing taped to Rebekah's arm and safety-pinned to the bedsheet. "This medicine will make you feel better," the nurse said, patting her patient.

When they were gone Leah stood and said, "I'll get you that cookie now."

Rebekah clutched at her. "Don't go, Leah. Please don't leave me."

Leah started to explain that she'd be right back, but the look of terror in Rebekah's eyes stopped her. "I won't leave," she said softly. "I won't leave you alone tonight for a single minute."

THREE

As she tried to fall asleep that night, Leah's mind flashed to a memory of when she was six years old. She and her mother had been living in a trailer, and Don, her mother's second husband, had been gone for more than a month. Her mother had tucked bedcovers around Leah. "Don't leave, Mama," Leah had pleaded.

"I have to go to work, Leah. But all the doors will be locked and I'll be back before you get up in the morning for school."

"Don't go," Leah wailed.

"Hush! Stop that. I don't want to go, but I have to if we want to eat next week. Close your eyes and go to sleep."

Leah had lain stiff and unmoving in the dark, listening to her mother's car driving away into the night. Dogs howled. Trees rustled in the wind. Terror made her heart pound until she thought it might pop out of her chest. She was alone. Totally alone . . .

"Leah?"

The sound of Rebekah's voice snapped Leah back to the present. "What?" she asked softly.

"Will you read me a story?"

"Um . . . I don't have a book." She remembered the library, but she doubted Rebekah would let her leave the room long enough to go there.

"I have my book." Rebekah pointed to the shelf in the bedside table.

Leah turned on the bedside light and retrieved a Bible storybook. "So, which story do you want to hear?"

"Read about Mary and the angel."

Leah rarely attended church and wasn't very familiar with the Bible, but she flipped open the well-worn book and scanned the table of contents. She found the story and read about how an angel of the Lord came to a young virgin to announce that she would bear God's Son. To Leah it had always sounded sort of farfetched. She knew virgins didn't get pregnant and remain virgins. Still, the story must have soothed Rebekah, because soon the little girl was asleep.

Leah stole back to her own bed and crawled between the sheets. Her knee again felt sore, and a nagging ache in her lower back made her toss restlessly. But she must have slept because she was startled awake when someone slid a blood pressure cuff around her arm.

"I'll be gone in a minute," the night nurse whispered.

"I only have a broken finger," Leah grumbled, irritated that she was being awakened to have her arm squeezed and a thermometer thrust in her mouth. Didn't these people have anything better to do than pester patients at night?

The night nurse performed the routine procedures on Rebekah too. Once the nurse had left the room, Leah heard Rebekah whimper. She called out, "Hey, it's okay. I'm right over here. Can you see me?"

"I'm scared, Leah."

Leah thought about getting up and going over to the child, but her back was sore and a draining fatigue was sapping her strength. "Do you want me to tell you a story?"

"Can you tell me about Abraham and Isaac?"

"Um . . . I'm afraid I don't know that one. How about *Snow White?*" she offered, reminding herself to leave out the scary parts about the witch.

"Who?" Rebekah asked.

Her question surprised Leah. She thought every little girl had seen the Disney version of the fairy tale. "How about *Cinderella* or *Sleeping Beauty?*"

"Who are they?"

Now Leah was at a loss. How could Rebekah not have heard these famous stories? "Never mind. How about I tell you all about where I used to live in Texas?"

"Is that far away?"

"Sure is." Leah started her story, describing the cowboys and Indians of legends—and wished she'd paid more attention in history class. In no time Rebekah drifted off to sleep.

Leah slept too, but she woke up when she heard someone come into the room. *Not another checkup,* she thought, moaning to herself. How did they expect a person to get well when the nurses kept waking her all night long? But the nurse didn't come to her bed. She went to Rebekah's. Through sleepy eyes Leah watched the woman smooth the sheets and tuck in the blankets around the sleeping child.

Her movements were whisper-soft, and she seemed so caring, so gentle, that a peaceful feeling washed over Leah. She was suddenly glad she wasn't alone in the farmhouse. At least in the hospital she could be near other people.

The nurse stood silently beside Rebekah's bed, and Leah drifted off to sleep.

She was awakened the next morning not by nurses but by doctors making rounds. Dr. Howser said, "Good morning, Leah. How are you feeling today?"

"Tired. Nurses kept coming in and out all night long."

He smiled. "Taking vital signs is hospital routine, I'm afraid. I want you to meet a colleague of mine."

He stepped aside, and another doctor peered down at her. "I'm Dr. Thomas, an orthopedist," the man said. "I'm a bone specialist and I've been called in to consult on your case."

"What's wrong with me?" she asked the tall, slim doctor.

He smiled reassuringly. "That's what we're going to find out. I've got a telephone conference scheduled with your parents this afternoon—"

"Neil's not my father," Leah interrupted.

"Sorry," Dr. Thomas said. "Anyway, Dr. Howser got your mother's approval to run some tests on you."

"What kinds of tests?" Leah was starting to feel uneasy.

"Blood work, of course. But also a CT bone scan."

"What's that? Will it hurt?"

"It's a kind of X ray that gives us a three-dimensional look at the inside of your body, and no, it doesn't hurt."

"Why would you want to see my bones?"

"To see what you're made of," he said with a twinkle in his eye.

"Sugar and spice and everything nice," she shot back, making him laugh. She quickly added, "Dr. Howser took an X ray of my finger yesterday. He said it was broken. What else is there to see?"

"The X ray showed that there was a small

hole in the bone. The hole weakened the finger and caused it to break. I want more X rays to confirm that finding. And I want to evaluate the condition of other bones in your body."

Neither doctor looked much concerned, which made Leah feel calmer. "So does this mean I'll be stuck in the hospital?"

"At least for a few days," Dr. Thomas said. "You've been staying by yourself at home, haven't you?"

She'd been staying by herself off and on since she was six, but she rarely told anyone that. People might get the impression that her mother was neglectful. She wasn't. But she *was* busy with her own life. "I can take care of myself," Leah told the doctors. "Mom's on her honeymoon, but she'll be back before Christmas."

"And we can reach her by phone," Dr. Howser assured his colleague.

Dr. Thomas flipped open Leah's chart. "You told Dr. Howser you've been tired lately."

"Sort of. But I've been busy too. I mean, this fall we moved up here, Mom got married, and I started a new school."

"Any other aches and pains?" He wrote as he talked.

"My knee's sore. And my back too."

"Where?"

She placed a hand against the small of her back. "Right here. Down deep. I think maybe I twisted it or something."

Dr. Thomas examined her, kneading her spine and manipulating her knee. She squirmed because the areas were sore and felt bruised. Finally he said, "Someone will come up later and take you down to X ray. And we'll see you again on rounds tomorrow morning."

When they were gone Leah looked over at Rebekah, who was staring at her. "Did they wake you up with all their talking?"

"I want my mama."

Leah wanted hers too, in a way. She smiled and said, "I'm sure she'll be back today for a visit."

Rebekah's lower lip began to tremble. Leah struggled out of bed and padded across the floor to Rebekah's bedside. The child's face still looked feverish, and her arm looked redder and more swollen. The IV bag was nearly empty. Leah wondered when Rebekah's doctor would be in to see her. "How about breakfast?" she asked, hoping to distract her. "I think I hear the cart coming down the hall."

Leah stopped talking because Rebekah didn't look interested. Her small shoulders began to shake, and sobs escaped from her mouth. Instinctively Leah put her arms around the girl. "Oh, Rebekah, don't cry," she begged, feeling helpless.

She saw the nurse call button and reached for it. But suddenly a male hand clamped over hers and a strong, firm voice boomed, "What are you doing to our sister?"

FOUR

Leah spun, only to stare up into the face of a tall blond-haired boy with intense sky-blue eyes.

"Ethan!" Rebekah cried. He scooped her up, and Leah stepped aside and bumped into a girl. She appeared to be Leah's age and was dressed in a simple long-sleeved brown dress. She wore a gauzy head covering identical to the one Rebekah's mother had been wearing.

The girl smiled and held out her hand. "I'm Charity Longacre, Rebekah's sister. You must be Leah. My parents spoke of you."

Thoroughly flustered, Leah eased backward toward her side of the room. She hadn't expected anyone from Rebekah's family to show up so early. Nor had she expected to face such a good-looking guy while she wore a shapeless hospital gown. She hadn't brushed her teeth either, or combed her hair or put on a smidgen of makeup. "It's so early," she mumbled.

"We left Nappanee, where we live, at five this morning. It's a hundred and fifty miles, and we didn't know what time breakfast would be served here in the hospital. We didn't want Rebekah to have to eat alone." Charity pulled off a cape and smoothed the long, full skirt of her dress. Her brown hair was parted in the middle and twisted into a bun. She wore no makeup, not even lipstick, but her green eyes were fringed with incredibly thick lashes, and her cheeks looked rosy from the cold outside.

Leah slid between the bedcovers and tugged them up to her chin, trying not to look as ill at ease as she felt. "Breakfast is on its way," she said.

Ethan turned, then averted his gaze from Leah in the bed. She saw color rush into his face and realized he was embarrassed by her presence. "I—I'm sorry if I spoke harshly to you," he said.

Harshly? Leah thought. *What a weird word for a teenage guy to use.* "No problem. Rebekah was crying, and I was just trying to calm her down."

"Where's Mama?" Rebekah asked.

"She'll be here later," Charity said. "After breakfast and morning chores. And she'll be bringing the baby so she won't have to rush home to nurse him."

"Who's feeding my chickens?" Rebekah asked.

"Simeon," Ethan said with an impish smile. "And not very gracefully either."

Rebekah giggled. Charity smiled at Leah and explained. "Simeon's seven and Rebekah took over hen duty from him last fall. He doesn't like taking up work in the henhouse again one bit."

"You have chickens?" Leah asked. Neil's farm had no animals, but what if he wanted them someday? Would she have to feed chickens and pigs? She didn't like the idea.

"We have many animals," Charity said. "Ours is a working farm, where our whole family lives."

"How many of you are there?"

"Mama and Papa, seven of us, and Opa and Oma, our grandparents, too."

"You *all* live in the same house? And you're

telling me Rebekah has *six* brothers and sisters?"

"There are three boys and four girls in our family," Charity said with pride. "Sarah's the oldest at nineteen. Ethan, seventeen"—she nodded toward her brother, who was sorting through a duffel bag with Rebekah—"me, I'm sixteen; our sister Elizabeth, she's twelve; Simeon; Rebekah; and Nathan, the baby, who's two months."

Leah had many friends in Dallas, but none had such a large family. While she sometimes wished she had a sister, she'd never wanted a whole bunch of sisters and brothers. In fact, when the kids she knew discussed large families, it was always with an air of disdain, as if too many siblings were an embarrassment. But Charity acted as if her large family were something to be proud of. "Sounds . . . large," Leah finally commented.

Charity laughed. "If the Lord wills it, most of the Amish have large families. Our house has been in our family for over seventy years, and one day it will go to Ethan because he's the oldest son. Right now we're getting ready for Christmas Day. Mama and Oma have been baking for weeks. And Papa and Opa are in the workshop late at night. I can't wait—"

"Charity!" Ethan barked. "We came to be with Rebekah, not bend the ears of her roommate."

Charity's face flushed beet red, and she dropped her gaze. "He's right. I'm sorry."

"She can talk the ears off of field corn," he said apologetically.

"I don't mind," Leah said. She thought the three of them were different and interesting. And she was lonely and wanted someone to talk to.

Just then an orderly entered, balancing breakfast trays. "Good morning." She set the trays down on utility tables in front of Leah and Rebekah.

Leah raised the cover on her plate and grimaced.

"What's wrong?" Charity asked.

"Eggs. *Ugh.* I hate eggs."

Charity studied her quizzically. "But you must eat breakfast?"

"I usually skip breakfast. Or I eat a muffin or fruit on my way to school."

"On the farm, I help Mama cook meals every day," Charity said. "We always have platters of bacon and eggs, hot biscuits, butter and honey before the men begin work in the fields."

"Well, sure," Leah said quickly. "I guess if you were going to plow the north forty you could eat that way. But most of us do other things all day. You know, like sit in school and listen to boring teachers."

"You don't like school?" Charity asked.

"It's so-so. Do you like it?"

"I no longer go to school. I completed my learning and now I help with the farm."

"You're finished with school?" Charity had sounded pleased with her achievement, but Leah was shocked. "How *can* you be?"

"Our bishop sees no purpose in school beyond eighth grade. Wisdom and understanding are much more important than knowledge and facts."

"Your *bishop* decides when you quit school?"

"I know all the important things," Charity countered. "I can calculate. I can read. I speak English and German. I have memorized many pages of Scripture. I know all that is necessary to be a wife and mother."

"A *what*?" Leah was stunned. "Don't you want to go to college?"

Ethan moved to stand beside his sister. "You

cannot go babbling to outsiders, sister. The English do not understand our ways. You make us sound foolish."

Leah felt a flash of anger. "You don't have to bite her head off. I mean, we're just talking. And I'm trying to understand your ways. Which sound pretty primitive to me."

The two Amish teens stepped back, as if Leah's anger had stung them. They both looked confused, and Leah was embarrassed. But it was Rebekah's cry that diverted everyone's attention.

"Don't yell at each other," she pleaded.

Both sister and brother turned and tried to console her.

"Are you mad at Leah?" Rebekah asked. "She is my friend. Don't be mad at her."

Leah felt her anger dissipate. "No one's mad," she said. "I'm sorry, Rebekah. I didn't mean to yell."

"And we're sorry too," Ethan said. He cast a glance at Leah. "Forgive me for speaking unkindly to you."

Leah shrugged, not trusting her own emotions. Ethan might have been one of the best-looking boys she'd ever met, but he was also the most unusual. She didn't know how to react to him.

Molly, the nurse from yesterday, breezed into the room. "Time for meds." She introduced herself to Rebekah, Ethan and Charity, checked Rebekah's IV and hung a new bag of clear fluid on the IV stand, chattering as she worked.

When she got to Leah, she said, "I'm supposed to take you down to X ray." She returned with a wheelchair, and when Leah protested, saying that she could walk, Molly shook her head. "No way. Every patient rides."

Leah was glad to get out of the room for a while and escape the tension her words with Ethan had caused. "Do you know anything about the Amish?" she asked Molly.

"A little. There's a large community of them up in Nappanee, along with a tourist attraction called Amish Acres. The Acres lets you take a peek at Amish life as it was a hundred years ago—which, incidentally, is about the same as it is today. These people live very simply. And they're not only exceptional farmers, they're also outstanding craftsmen, especially in carpentry work."

"Well, I think they're weird," Leah declared. "And I do mean *weird*."

"Not weird . . . just different. They call themselves plain people because they don't believe in adornments of any kind. They separate themselves from the rest of us, whom they call English—the out-worlders."

Leah recalled Ethan calling her "English" and "an outsider" back in the room. "They're plain, all right. Did you know that Charity doesn't even go to school because some bishop thinks she should just get married and have babies? Is that backward or what? I'll bet they treat women like slaves."

"You're wrong. The Old Order Amish have built their lifestyle on the values of love, forgiveness and peace. They're such pacifists that Congress has exempted Amish men from military service. Mostly they just want to be left alone."

Leah shook her head. "Doesn't sound like much fun to me. What's wrong with civilization?"

"Plenty, to their way of thinking. They believe the outside world will contaminate their culture and change them and their ways. They avoid such contamination at all costs."

"But if that's so, then everything in this place is a contaminant." It unsettled Leah to think of herself that way.

Molly stopped the wheelchair in front of a door marked "Radiation Lab." "Well, fortunately they aren't against modern medicine. Good thing too. Rebekah is one very sick little girl."

FIVE

Molly's statement sobered Leah. "She is? All she told me was that a spider bit her."

"Yes, a brown recluse spider. That can be bad enough, but now a strep or staph infection has set in and is moving up her arm from the site of the bite. Her doctor's got her on a powerful IV antibiotic. That's why she's in the hospital."

Leah was worried about Rebekah. And she felt protective of the child, although there was no need for that with Ethan around.

A technician stepped up to Leah. "You ready?"

She started, having forgotten for a moment why she was there. "I'm ready," she said.

"I'll come back for you," said Molly as she left the room.

The technician wheeled Leah into a small lab. "First thing we do is inject a little radioactive fluid into you," he said. "Your bones absorb it and then show up nice and clear on the film."

After the injection Leah had to kill time in a tiny waiting room that had been decorated for Christmas. Candy canes and glass balls were strung on a tinsel garland hanging along one wall, and a tiny artificial tree with blinking lights sat on a TV set. A lopsided angel perched atop the tree. One of her wings was bent. Leah felt a wave of self-pity sweep through her. She'd just as soon skip Christmas this year. The holiday was all tinsel and glitz and had no meaning.

The technician returned and led her into a room with a table and an enormous machine with a flat, glasslike plate. "This is the camera," he explained. "You climb up on the table, lie flat and be still. The camera will move along your body and photograph your skeleton one part at a time. This will give your doctor a look at your entire bone structure."

"What's my doctor looking for, anyway?"

The technician shrugged. "You'll have to ask him. All I do is take the pictures." He settled her on the table and left the room. Soon his voice came through a speaker. "All ready?"

"Let's do it."

The huge camera moved with a mechanical clunking down her body. After a short time the technician announced, "All done."

Leah returned to the wheelchair and waited for Molly. It seemed as if she sat there forever. Just when she'd decided to wheel herself back up to her floor, Molly hurried into the room, visibly upset. "Leah, I'm so sorry! I didn't mean to leave you stranded down here, but we've had a minor disaster on the floor."

"What kind? Flood? Tornado? Fire? Is everyone okay?"

"Nothing like that. Someone stole the Christmas tree for the pedi floor."

"Stole it?"

"It's a big artificial tree, a really good one. We take it down every year and put it in the same storage room. But this year when we went to haul it out, it was missing."

"Sort of like the Grinch stealing Christmas."

"Worse. If I ever find out who did it . . ."

"So what're you going to do about a tree?"

"Well, we're taking up a collection to buy a new one so we won't have to postpone tomorrow night's decorating party."

"I could put in a few dollars," Leah said, thinking of Rebekah. She wondered if Amish children had ever heard of Santa Claus.

Molly patted her shoulder. "Patients shouldn't have to help bankroll a Christmas tree. But thanks for the offer."

When Leah returned to her room, Charity was sitting in a chair beside Rebekah's bed, knitting. Ethan wasn't there. Rebekah was sleeping, so Charity pulled the curtain that separated Rebekah's and Leah's beds and took a chair over to Leah's side of the room. "Would you like to sit and talk?" she asked.

"Where's the watchdog?" Leah asked.

Charity giggled. "You mean Ethan? He's exploring. Neither of us has ever been to a hospital before."

"Hospitals are pretty boring. Especially when you feel fine." Leah filled Charity in about what was going on with her medically. "Basically, they aren't telling me anything."

"They will tell your parents, won't they?"

"My mother," Leah corrected. "Neil's not my father."

"Doesn't your real father know you're in the hospital?"

"No. He died when I was ten."

Charity looked startled. "Oh—I'm so sorry, Leah. You've never even known your own father?"

Her words stung, but Leah quickly realized that Charity was only curious. From the viewpoint of Charity's supertight family, a family with no father might seem as strange as a two-headed dog. "He took off when I was three. My name, Lewis-Hall, is the last name of both my parents put together."

"My mother took my father's name," Charity said. "I thought every woman took her husband's name."

"Lots of people hyphenate last names. And some women don't change their names at all. If I took a new last name every time my mother remarried, my name would be a foot long."

"How many times has she married?"

"Neil is number five." Charity looked so shocked, Leah felt compelled to explain. "But she's done better every time. You know, some women work for a living, some marry." All at once she felt foolish under Charity's incredulous stare. "Well, don't Amish women ever remarry?" she asked.

"Only if they are widowed."

"You don't believe in divorce?"

"Under some circumstances it is allowed, but marriage is a holy union. It is a covenant, like the one God made with his people. It should not be broken."

Leah rolled her eyes indulgently. "Not anymore. Don't you know what's going on in today's world?"

"No. And I'm not sure I want to know."

Charity's naïveté was beginning to get on Leah's nerves. "Well, here's a news flash: People don't stay in bad marriages anymore."

"People think we are strange because we choose to be the way we are," Charity said softly. "But what's normal about taking many spouses and not having a family home?"

Leah stiffened. "Different strokes for different folks."

Charity studied her with her clear green eyes until Leah began to feel squirmy. She decided to change the subject. "Um—so, how's Rebekah?"

Charity's brow puckered. "Not so good."

Leah sat up straighter. "She's not improving?"

"It's slow. But many people are praying for her—" She stopped abruptly.

"It's all right. You don't have to watch every word you say around me. I had friends back in Dallas who prayed."

"But you don't?"

"I just never got into religion." Now Leah felt self-conscious about her lack of sophistication in a world that Charity knew intimately. "Maybe we shouldn't talk about this stuff. I—I like you and I don't want to say anything more to hurt your feelings."

Charity's face broke into a generous smile. "I like you, too, Leah Lewis-Hall. I have never had an outsider friend."

An outsider. That's what Leah had been all her life. She and her mother had moved so often, she'd never felt as if she belonged anywhere. And despite the defiant confidence she showed Charity, she was embarrassed by her mother's five marriages. Why couldn't her mother just get it right so that they could live like regular people?

Leah asked, "So is your mother coming later today?"

"She can't. I haven't told Rebekah yet because it will upset her. Baby Nathan is sick with a fever, and Mama must stay with him. Papa is coming tomorrow—Saturday. Until then Ethan and I will have to substitute for our parents."

"Maybe you could call your mother later tonight and let Rebekah talk to her."

"We have no phone."

"You're kidding!"

"None of the Amish where we live have phones."

"But how did your mother let you know about the baby?"

"She went into town and used the phone. We are not opposed to using phones, we just do not believe in owning them."

This made no sense to Leah. "But if you use phones, why not have one in your house?"

Charity smiled patiently and, leaning forward, said, "We have no electricity, no cars, no modern things. Life on our farms is as it was a hundred years ago. The Bible says that Christians should separate themselves from the world, that we should be 'in the world, but not *of* the world.' We 'hold fast to that which is good.' For us, faith is lived out in our community. We marry our own kind, birth our own kind, bury our own kind.

"We believe that God created all things and that he sustains all creation. We believe that man is sinful and that only the blood of Jesus can redeem us from our sins. We expect to die and go to heaven and glorify God forever. We are not like you, Leah. But also, we are not backward, or stupid, or foolish. We are Amish. And I am not ashamed."

Leah listened dumbstruck. Charity was so certain of what she believed that she could speak about it without stumbling over words. And without apology, Leah knew she should respond but she didn't know how. The sudden buzz of the phone rescued her. Quickly she rose to answer it before it could ring again and wake Rebekah.

"Hello?"

"Leah, darling! Neil spoke with your doctors just an hour ago. Can we talk?"

SIX

"I'm stuck in the hospital, remember?" Leah replied. "What else is there to do but talk?" She held her hand over the mouthpiece and told Charity, "It's my mother."

Charity waved and slipped behind Rebekah's curtain.

From faraway Japan, her mother's voice said, "Don't act sulky, Leah. You're being cared for."

But not by you, Leah thought. "So what did the doctor tell you?" she asked.

"Not a darn thing! Honestly, I hope they know what they're doing at that place. You'd think they could tell us something by now."

Leah was disappointed. "They still don't know what's wrong with me?"

"Evidently, according to Dr. Thomas," her mother said, then quoted, "you're 'manifesting symptoms that are consistent with any number of health problems.' As if that's supposed to pacify me. At any rate, they've scheduled more tests starting Monday morning, and once they can evaluate the results, they *might* be able to diagnose you. There's no excuse for dragging this thing out."

"I don't want to spend Christmas in the hospital."

"I'm sure you won't have to. But until I get some sort of definitive word from your doctor, I'm not cutting my honeymoon short. That seemed okay with you the last time we talked."

"Sure, it's fine." Leah forced herself not to sound disappointed.

"But don't you worry. We're flying into Indianapolis December twenty-third, just like we planned. We'll come straight to the hospital and spring you. Then it's home to the farm for Christmas Eve and Christmas Day. We'll put up a tree and put out all our presents. Why, I'm even planning to cook a turkey with all the trimmings."

"But what if they still don't know what's wrong with me?"

"Then we'll find another doctor after Christmas. But I'm sure that won't be necessary. Now, is there anything else we need to discuss?"

Leah could think of a hundred things. She wanted to say "I'm scared" but couldn't get the words out. She wanted to say "I love you."

"Um, Mom, I—"

"Whoops! Sorry, dear, I've got to run. Someone's at the door. I'll call you before Monday. *Ciao*."

Leah held the receiver for a long time, listening to the dial tone that only moments before had been the voice of her mother. With tears welling in her eyes, she hung up.

She decided to take a belated morning shower and put on her makeup, hoping it would make her feel better. She was just adding the finishing touches—not easy with her broken finger—when Molly came in to take blood pressures and temps. By now Rebekah was awake, but she lay in the bed listlessly. She looked feverish. Charity tried to soothe her while Molly worked.

"Did you find the missing tree?" Leah

asked, coming out of the bathroom as she spritzed on an expensive perfume.

"Still missing," Molly said.

Leah told Charity what had happened.

"Stealing is wrong," Charity said, sighing. "This outsider world of yours is not a very nice place, Leah."

Was she asking Leah to defend the world at large? "There are good people too," Leah said. "Aren't there, Molly?"

"A few saints. An angel or two."

"Where's the angel?" Rebekah asked.

"The angels are watching over you, little sister. You just can't see them," said Charity, smoothing Rebekah's damp forehead.

"Can you see any angels, Leah?" Rebekah asked.

"Not really." Believing in angels was a little like believing in fairies and elves, Leah thought. Interesting mythology, but not scientifically valid.

Molly said, "I think *you're* an angel, Rebekah. Now, why don't you close your eyes and let this good medicine do its work." She adjusted the drip on Rebekah's IV.

Rebekah sighed. Molly turned to Leah. "You look pretty. Got a date?"

Leah ran her fingers through her thick hair. "Actually, I think I missed my date with the lunch tray. I'm starved."

"My fault," Molly said. "I didn't get you back up here in time. But don't worry, there's plenty to eat in the rec room. Pizza, sandwiches, fresh fruit—go help yourself."

"Do you want me to bring you something?" Leah asked Charity.

"No, thank you. We ate already." Charity smiled at Leah.

The rec room was more crowded than before. The giant-screen TV was now showing *The Little Mermaid* for a group of engrossed kids, as toddlers climbed on the plastic play equipment. Some of the children were hooked to IV lines that hung from poles standing next to them. Some were bald from chemotherapy treatments. Some had broken limbs in casts. A candy striper aide sat in a corner, overseeing the group and running interference when two toddlers had a confrontation.

Leah ventured into the kitchen and stopped short. Ethan stood in front of a vending machine, contemplating the selections.

"You have to put money in. You can't just

wish the stuff out," Leah said, hoping to make him smile.

Startled, he jumped back. "You surprised me." His cheeks reddened, and he dropped his gaze. He didn't offer her the hoped-for smile.

"Sorry," she said irritably. Why did he always look away from her? Did his religion forbid him to look her in the eye? "Do you want me to help?" she asked.

"I—I have no money for the machine."

"I have quarters." She reached into the pocket of her robe. "Here. Let me treat you. What would you like?"

"I cannot take—"

"Of course you can," she interrupted. "Buying you a candy bar doesn't make us engaged, does it?" She popped in two quarters. "What's your favorite?"

"I don't know. I've never had one before."

"Are you joking?"

"Is this funny to you?"

"Only strange," she said, more hesitant now, her annoyance subsiding. "I'll pick for you." She punched a button, and a Milky Way bar dropped down the chute. She picked it up and handed it to him. "This is one of my favorites. Try it."

Hesitantly he took it from her, careful not to touch her hand. "Thank you."

She tried to make eye contact, but Ethan kept his gaze on the candy bar. Again her anger flared. She spun and stalked over to the counter and a platter holding a stack of wrapped sandwiches. She grabbed one, took a fruit drink, and dropped into a nearby chair, pointedly ignoring Ethan. The guy might be good-looking, but he was a jerk as far as she was concerned.

From the corner of her eye she saw that Ethan hadn't left the room. He just stood by the door, shifting from foot to foot. His shirt was white broadcloth. His pants were the same wide-legged style as his father's. He wore heavy, dark boots. There was nothing fashionable about him. He was nothing like any of the boys she'd known back in Dallas. She tried hard not to look at him. Still he didn't move.

She couldn't stand it anymore. "What!" she cried. "What do you want? Is the candy bar poison or something?"

He shook his head, his gaze riveted to the floor.

"Then what's wrong, Ethan? Is there something wrong with me? Is there a particular reason why you won't look at me or talk to me?"

"No." He came closer until he was standing over her, staring straight down into her eyes.

His gaze was so intense that Leah felt as if it might burn her. She swallowed hard. Her hands trembled, and her heart began to race. "What is it? Do you dislike me?" Her voice quivered with false bravado.

"Dislike you?" He looked as if she'd slapped him. "I do not dislike you, Leah Lewis-Hall. I think that you are the most beautiful girl I have ever set my eyes upon."

SEVEN

"You do?" Leah stared at him. "You actually think I'm pretty?"

"It is impossible for me not to think so. You *are* beautiful."

She felt herself blush. No guy had ever been so forthright with her. In her experience, most guys liked to play head games with girls. They liked to come on strong, then back away if a girl showed any interest. She grew wary. Maybe Ethan was the same way. "I'll bet you've told lots of girls they're pretty," she said tentatively.

He shook his head. "I have only taken Martha Dewberry home but once in my buggy."

"You've lost me, Ethan. What's a buggy ride got to do with feeding girls a line?" Leah pushed out a nearby chair with her foot, inviting Ethan to sit.

He sat. "What is this 'feeding a line'?"

"Giving somebody a compliment in order to get something you want from her." She wondered if she was going to have to explain every idiom in the English language to him.

"You mean *lie*?" He recoiled. "I do not lie, Leah. If I tell you you are beautiful, it is because it is so."

She couldn't help smiling. "Well, thank you for thinking so. I would have never guessed you felt that way. You acted as if you wanted to avoid me. That can hurt a person's feelings, you know."

"Have I hurt your feelings?"

"I'm getting over it."

A smile slowly inched across Ethan's face. "Good. I do not want to hurt your feelings."

She measured him quietly. Ethan's hands were large and raw; he must work hard. His face was lean, with the hint of a beard in places. His hair curled against his collar and flopped appealingly across his forehead. She wanted to touch it, but she didn't dare. She asked, "Are you going to tell me about Martha Dewberry and your buggy ride together?"

He regarded Leah seriously. "It is our custom that when a man is interested in a woman, he takes her home from church or community gatherings in a buggy. It is his way of telling others that he has special feelings for this person."

Despite herself, Leah felt a tiny flare of jealousy. "Where I come from, if a guy likes a girl, he asks her out on a date and he picks her up in his car. Or his parents' car."

"We have no cars."

"That's what your sister told me. But you don't mind riding in them."

"Public transportation is fine for long trips, but for each one of us to own a car would be prideful. And it would break apart our community."

Every family Leah knew owned a car. Sometimes two or three cars. Neil had given her mother a car for a wedding gift, and Leah had used it to drive herself to the hospital. But she could see how vehicles separated people. She thought of people driving on the expressways, each locked alone inside a car, cut off from fellow travelers. "So, are you a good buggy driver?"

He grinned. "Passable."

"And do you like this Martha Dewberry? Is she your girlfriend?"

His brow puckered while his gaze lingered over Leah's face. "She is Amish."

And I'm not. She heard the unspoken message in his comment. Suddenly she wanted to turn the talk away from their differences. She liked Ethan. But nothing could ever come of their friendship; they were from two very different worlds. She moved forward. "I'll bet you've never played a video game, have you?"

He shook his head. "I have not ever seen one."

She grabbed his hand. "Come on. Let me show you how."

She led him into the semidarkened video game room. Several kids clustered around machines, but she saw a vacant one back in a corner and took Ethan toward it. "Sit," she directed. She positioned herself across the table from him. "I've played this one before back in Texas. It's got levels of difficulty, so we can start slow, until you get the hang of it." She paused, suddenly stricken by a thought. "It wouldn't be against your religion, would it?"

His features glowed by the pale purple light emanating from the game. "Play is not forbidden. We play many games. I can see no harm in trying this one."

It didn't take him long to catch on. Ethan's hand flew on the trackball, spinning and turning it. Leah threw up her hands in defeat as he soared over the million-point mark. "Are you sure you've never played a video game before? If I didn't know better, I'd bet you'd suckered me."

His face was lit with a heart-stopping grin of genuine pleasure. "What do you mean—'suckered'?"

"You know, *pretended* not to know how to play."

"I told you, Leah, I do not lie." His eyes twinkled. "It is an exciting game. I like it."

"You have to admit that modern conveniences aren't all bad."

He leveled his incredibly blue eyes on her. "They have their pleasures."

A tingling sensation prickled up her arms. "Too bad you need electricity to play it."

He laughed. "Electricity is not the only need.

Time is necessary too. With so much to do on the farm, who would have time for video games?"

"It seems to me that work is all you have time for."

"Work is a good teacher. It gives us Amish a sense of meaning and purpose."

"Does it give *you* meaning?"

He pondered her question, and she hoped he could tell that she was genuinely interested in his perspective.

"Work helps me understand that my life is but one small part of God's greater order," he said. "The seasons come. They go. Harvest comes, and with it, God supplies our needs. But if we did nothing but *wish* for a good harvest, if we did no work to produce a good crop, then that would be foolish. And worse, it would presume on God's benevolence."

Presented that way, his point of view made perfect sense to Leah. "Don't you ever get curious about the rest of the world, though?"

She could tell she'd hit a nerve. For all of his confidence about his lifestyle, there was yearning too. And by the way he played the video game, she guessed, there was intense competitiveness. "I cannot tell you otherwise, Leah.

Yes, I do wonder what certain things would be like among you English. Since I've been here in this hospital, I have seen many people who care and who help others. Like Amish ways.

"But I have also seen your newspapers and your television programs since I've been here. They tell terrible stories about your world. People kill others to steal their cars—even when they have cars of their own." He shook his head. "This is not a world where I want to live."

Leah couldn't deny that horrible things went on in the world every day. "All right, I agree. The world's not a perfect place. But why not try to change it instead of hiding from it?"

He shook his head. "The elders tell us that it is far more likely that the English will change our ways than that we will change theirs."

"Do you always do what the elders say?" Both he and Charity quoted rules and words of others. Did they ever think for themselves?

"*Gelassenheit*," he said. "That's German for patience and resignation. It means obedience to the Amish community. It is not something we *do*. It is something we *are*."

Leah had been raised to be on her own. Her mother's many marriages, their frequent moves and different schools had taught her to be independent. But she saw quite clearly that for the Amish, individuality was not a virtue. It was a curse. She stood. "Well, it looks like we've come full circle, Ethan. You were right after all—the English and the Amish can't mingle."

He stood too. "But we can care about one another," he said carefully. "We can always care."

She knew he meant *care* in a brotherly way. But after spending time with him, she didn't want to be just another sister to him. She wanted to be a girl who mattered to him the way Martha Dewberry mattered. Except that Leah wasn't Amish. And she never would be.

That evening, Leah overheard Ethan tell his sisters that he was returning home on a shuttle bus. Rebekah reacted immediately, asking him not to leave her and Charity. Leah reacted too, but quietly, deep inside herself. She knew she was going to miss him.

"Papa needs me to work, but I will be back," Ethan said.

"When?"

"Tomorrow evening. By suppertime."

Leah's heartbeat accelerated. *Good. He's com-*

ing back. When he left the room, he passed the table where she sat, trailed his fingers across the surface and softly brushed her arm. She met his gaze and felt a rush of yearning. She wanted to stand up and throw her arms around him. Instead, she sat perfectly still.

She was preparing to go to bed when Dr. Thomas came into the room. Leah was surprised to see him there so late on a Friday night. "I got tied up in the emergency room with a leg fracture; that's why I'm so late making rounds," he explained.

"I'm not going anywhere." She felt apprehensive. "So, do you know anything about what's wrong with me yet?"

He shuffled her chart, laden with X rays and papers. "I know that I want to do a biopsy on your knee first thing Monday morning."

EIGHT

"Why do you have to do a biopsy?" Leah asked Dr. Thomas.

"A biopsy is nothing more than a diagnostic tool—"

Leah cut him off. "I *know* what a biopsy is! That's how the doctors discovered that my grandmother had cancer." She gasped. "Do you think I have cancer? Is that why you want to do a biopsy?"

"Now, calm down. There are some cancers that have a hereditary factor, but that doesn't necessarily mean you have cancer. I don't want to make a false diagnosis, and since we don't know what's wrong with you yet, I want to do this test. I'll put you under an anesthetic, take out a tiny sample of bone tissue from your knee, and send it to the lab for evaluation. Your knee might be sore for a day or two, but that's all."

Leah felt afraid. "Do whatever you have to."

The doctor patted her arm. "You'll be okay, Leah. We'll take good care of you. I'll see you Monday morning." He smiled reassuringly as he left.

Leah pulled the bedcovers up to her chin and closed her eyes. She didn't want Charity or Rebekah to see the tears that were about to roll down her cheeks as, for the first time since entering the hospital, she surrendered completely to memories of her grandmother.

Grandma Hall had tried to stay involved in Leah's life even after Leah's father had abandoned them. It wasn't easy. For reasons Leah still didn't understand, her mother had tried to keep Leah away from her grandmother. Her mother didn't want Grandma Hall to see Leah at all. But Grandma Hall found ways to keep in touch. She sent Leah letters, even when they lived in the same city, and whenever she could, she stopped by Leah's school during recess to visit.

Leah remembered her grandmother as

cheerful and smiling. She carried hankies that smelled like roses, and she loved to wear red. Most importantly, she was Leah's only tie to her father—the father her mother wouldn't allow her to mention. The father Leah longed for, instead of the steady stream of men who had dated her mother.

Leah's grandmother had told her stories about her father when he was a little boy and showed her photos of him as a child, as a soldier in Vietnam, as a new father proudly holding baby Leah. And when she'd ask, "Why did my daddy go away?" Grandma Hall would say, "He just had to go, honey. But he always loved you. And he still does."

When Leah was ten, Grandma Hall had gotten sick, and Leah's mother had relented slightly about allowing Leah to visit her. Although feelings between the two were strained, Leah's mother had often brought Leah to the hospital. "Hi, darling," her grandmother would say, and she would stroke Leah's hair tenderly.

Leah had hated the hospital. Her grandmother looked awful, gaunt and pale, with IVs stuck into bulging blue veins. Leah hated the way the place smelled and feared the equipment, tubes, and syringes, as well as the nurses who shuffled in and out, dispensing medicine but bringing her beloved grandmother no relief. Secretly Leah hoped one day to walk in and see her father visiting his mother. But it had never happened.

Grandma Hall lived three months from the time she was diagnosed. She might have survived longer, except that one day when Leah and her mother went to visit, Grandma Hall was sobbing uncontrollably. "He's dead, Roberta. My boy's dead. I got a letter from some hospital out in Oregon. They found him unconscious in an alley."

That was when Leah knew her father was gone forever. And after that, Grandma Hall went downhill quickly. She died, a shadow of herself, hooked to machines, in pain, alone in the hospital.

And now, Leah thought, *here I am, all alone, in a hospital.* Grandma Hall, if she had been here, would have held Leah's hand and told her not to worry, that she'd protect her. But Grandma Hall was dead. That left Leah's mother—and tender loving care had never been one of her strong suits.

Leah wiped her eyes with the edge of her bedsheet and rolled over. Charity was preparing for bed on a roll-away cot that had been brought into the room. "How's Rebekah?" Leah asked.

"Her fever's down." Charity was wearing a long nightdress of cotton flannel, and her light brown hair hung down her back in a long braid. "And the swelling on her arm has gone down too. I have prayed for these things to happen. And I have asked God to let her go home in time for Christmas. It wouldn't be the same without all of us together."

"Are you trying to tell me you believe your prayers made her well, and not the medicine she's been taking?"

"Of course the medicine helped her. But prayer is strong medicine too. Sometimes it is all we have when nothing else works."

"You know, I want Rebekah to get well, but I'm going to miss the two of you when you leave." And Ethan too, she thought.

"What did your doctor tell you?" Charity asked. Leah explained about the biopsy. "I will say extra prayers for you that this biopsy gives your doctor the answer he is looking for," said Charity.

They told one another "Good night," and Leah switched off the light over her bed. Dim

light from the hallway leaked under the bottom
of the door, and the wall switches glowed in
the dark. As her eyes adjusted, Leah could see
Charity kneeling beside her bed, her hands
folded and her head bowed. The simplicity of
the pose brought a lump to Leah's throat. She
wondered if there really was a God after all.
Then she thought of her beloved Grandma
Hall, dying in the hospital. Leah was touched
by Charity's taking the time to pray on her
behalf. But nothing had helped her grandma
when she was sick: not prayers; not doctors;
and not all the love Leah held in her heart for
her. What could possibly help Leah?

Leah was awakened by a night nurse for vitals, but long after the nurse had left the room,
she remained awake. She kept thinking about
Ethan and how attracted she was to him, in
spite of his simple and unsophisticated ways.
Maybe that was what attracted her. He was
singleminded and focused, confident of what
he believed, positive of the direction his life
would take.

Leah couldn't say any of those things about
herself. She meandered through school, doing
just enough work to get by. She'd vaguely

thought about college, but only because it seemed like the thing to do, not because there was anything particular she wanted to study or learn. Yet she didn't want to be like her mother either, drifting from place to place, marrying and remarrying, always searching for something more or better or just different.

Leah sighed. All this thinking wasn't helping her go back to sleep. She turned over. With a start, she saw a woman standing beside Rebekah's bed. *When did she come into the room?* Leah peered through the gloom and recognized her as the nurse who'd come in the night before. The woman leaned over Charity's cot and smoothed her covers. Then she went to Rebekah's bed and took the child's small hand in hers. Leah heard Rebekah giggle quietly, then begin animatedly whispering with the nurse.

Watching the scene, Leah realized this nurse really had a way with children. And Molly had certainly done a lot to make Leah feel cared for and comfortable. *Nursing.* Maybe that would be something she'd like doing. Leah toyed with the notion, turned it over in her mind, and discovered that she liked it.

Leah continued to watch the night nurse and

Rebekah whispering, and slowly a calming peace stole over her. Her eyelids grew heavy, and as the silence of the night closed around her, she fell fast asleep.

"I'm hungry." Rebekah's voice woke Leah and Charity.

Leah rubbed the sleep from her eyes and saw the little girl sitting up in bed with her doll in her lap. Morning sunlight flooded the room. "Are you okay, Rebekah?" she asked.

"Yes, but I am hungry."

Charity got out of bed and scurried to Rebekah's bedside. She felt her forehead with the back of her hand. "I think her fever is gone." She flashed Leah a smile. "It seems she is well."

"That's a relief!"

Molly walked through the doorway. "What's a relief?"

"We think Rebekah's much better," Leah said.

"I'm hungry," Rebekah repeated.

"That's a good sign," Molly said with a grin. "The breakfast trays are on their way, so let's get a temp before you eat." She slid a digital thermometer under Rebekah's tongue. While she was waiting for the readout, she asked Leah, "Did you sleep well?"

"Except for when the nurses came for vitals in the middle of the night. I didn't think I'd ever get back to sleep. Then another nurse came in, and watching her and Rebekah must have made me sleepy, because the next thing I knew it was morning."

"What other nurse?"

"Gabriella," Rebekah said around the thermometer. "She's my friend. She comes in and talks to me."

"Gabriella? She must be brand new."

"She's nice," said Rebekah.

"Well, it must be nice to have that much free time." Molly removed the thermometer when it beeped. "But that's the difference between the day and night shifts. Maybe I'll switch and not have so much work to do."

"Who'll I talk to all day?" Leah kidded.

Molly chuckled, turned to Charity and said, "Good news. Your sister's temperature is normal."

Charity clapped. "Wonderful! When can she go home?"

"Not until her doctor says she can. Infections

can be ornery. We want to be sure it's truly gone before we release her."

Leah thought of how lonely it would be without company in the room. "Are you leaving me, Rebekah?"

Rebekah's face puckered. "Oh, Leah, you are my best-ever friend. I'll come visit you. Won't we, Charity?"

Everyone laughed, but Leah knew that once the two girls were gone, they wouldn't be back. Leah doubted that Charity's parents would allow her to make the trip again when there was no reason other than a social call.

Later that morning, after Leah had showered, washed her hair, and put on makeup, she went to the library on the pediatric floor and checked out some books about nursing. She was reading at the table in her room when Ethan came in, smiling.

Rebekah squealed with delight. Ethan beamed at his sisters, then cast a sparkling blue-eyed glance at Leah. "I told you I would return. And guess what? I have brought you all a big surprise."

NINE

"A surprise? What is it? Tell me, Ethan." Rebekah was bubbling over with excitement.

"Papa is downstairs with it."

"I want to see Papa!"

"You will in just a little bit. After he takes care of delivering the surprise."

"Am I included in your surprise?" Leah asked, smiling.

"Yes," Ethan said, turning his clear blue eyes on her.

"What is it?"

His sisters were asking the same question, but he didn't take his gaze off Leah's face as he answered, "It is a Christmas tree to take the place of the one that was stolen. Papa and I cut it early this morning from the woods."

"*Our* woods?" Charity asked, sounding astonished.

"Yes."

"A *Christmas* tree?"

"Yes."

Leah hadn't a clue why Charity was so surprised, nor did she really care. She only knew that gazing into Ethan's eyes was making her heart pound and her pulse race.

Molly hurried into the room. "The front desk says there's a man with a Christmas tree down in the lobby. He says his name is Longacre and he wants to bring it up to the rec room."

Ethan turned. "Our papa. I told him of the theft and he said he would like to bring a tree for the children. We cut it, and a trucker from town helped us get it here."

"We—all of us nurses—are so grateful, Ethan. Yes, have him bring it up in the freight elevator. I'll call a custodian to help."

Ethan left, and Leah and Molly followed him. "It's pretty nice of them to bring the floor a tree, but why is it such a big deal?" Leah asked.

"The Amish don't celebrate Christmas the way we do," Molly said. "They never decorate Christmas trees, and they never focus on exchanging lots of Christmas presents."

"Then why are they doing this?"

Molly shrugged. "You'll have to ask Ethan."

In the rec room, everyone was waiting for the tree delivery. Before long, a handcart carrying the giant evergreen burst through the doorway. Guided by the custodian and steadied by Ethan and his father, the tree was enormous, so tall that it scraped the ceiling. Ice clung to a few of its branches.

"It's wonderful!" Molly cried. She and a group of nurses had gathered at the door to watch.

"Where do you want it?" the custodian asked.

Nurses scurried to make a place for it in a corner of the room. Leah watched Ethan help set the tree in a bucket of water and anchor it down. She couldn't take her eyes off him. His forearms bulged with exertion, and his shirt stretched taut across his back. In minutes the tree stood securely, its pungent pine scent filling the room.

"It did not seem so large in the woods," Ethan's father said.

"It's perfect. Thank you so much, Mr. Longacre. The kids will love it," Leah heard Molly say. "I hope we have enough decorations for it. We'll go ahead with the decorating party after all." She turned to one of the nurses. "Call the cafeteria. Tell them what's going on and see if they can't rustle up some cookies, or some kind of Christmas goodies."

The crowd began to break up.

"Now, I am going to see my daughters," Jacob told his son. Charity had remained in the room with Rebekah.

"I will come shortly, Papa," Ethan said.

When they were alone, Leah walked over to him. "This was very nice of you. But Molly said the Amish don't make a big fuss over Christmas."

"Christmas is important to us, Leah. It is the day Christ was born."

"But it's different for you than it is for us. Why did you bring the tree?"

"It is true that our ways are not your ways, but Christmas is special for us. In our house we exchange gifts. Not all Amish do, but we do. It is a day of feasting and visiting and being with our family."

"But we're not in your family. We're 'English.'"

"I told Papa of all the children who can't go home for Christmas Day. I told him how much the Christmas tree means to them."

"So this is just an act of Christian charity?" Leah wasn't sure how she felt about that.

"It is a kindness, yes. But it is also a way of bringing *you* a little of my farm and home. The woods are very beautiful and the trees have stood there many years. I wish you could see them."

Leah had already begun to grasp Ethan's deep love for the earth and living things. She understood that giving up the tree had not been done lightly. "I wish I could see them too." She bent several needles of the tree and released more of the heavy pine aroma. "But I guess this is the only way I'll ever go there."

He didn't say anything, and she felt her heart sink a little. Their worlds were far apart, and there was nothing she could do to bridge the gap. He was Amish. She was English.

"Did you hear that Rebekah's fever broke this morning?"

"It did? That's wonderful. I will go see her right away." Halfway to the door he asked, "Are you coming with me?"

"Not now. I'll let all of you visit together for a while."

"But it's your room too."

But not my family, she thought. "Go on. I'll come later." Suddenly she panicked at the thought of his leaving without her seeing him again. "Will you stay for the party tonight?"

"Papa wants to go right home. There are chores to do, work that can't wait. And tomorrow is Sunday, the Sabbath. That is a day for rest and for church and family. Charity and I will both leave . . ." He let his sentence trail off. "But this is probably not interesting to you. Forgive me."

Everything about him was interesting to her. "I—I'll miss all of you when you leave for good."

"And I shall miss you, Leah."

The sound of her name on his lips made her heart flutter. "But you'll be back on Monday?"

"Is this important to you?"

She told him about her biopsy. "I—I think it would be easier if I knew someone was going to be with me when I woke up from the anesthesia. It's no big deal. Just a nice thing to know."

A wry smile turned up the corners of Ethan's mouth. "I think, Leah Lewis-Hall, that you are not so brave as you sometimes pretend."

Leah squared her chin. "I'm used to being alone. I just thought . . . forget it. I don't want you to put yourself out or anything."

"Put myself out?"

"It means—"

"I know what it means. I cannot understand how you would think that it would be a bother to me to be here when you wake up from your surgery. You are not a bother, Leah. You are special."

The way he said the word *special,* the way he was looking at her, made her want to throw herself into his arms. "That's nice of you to say."

"I did not say it to be nice. I said it because it is true."

"And you don't lie."

He grinned. "You know me well."

She returned a smile. "You'd better go visit with Rebekah before your father comes looking for you."

"Don't stay away too long," he said as he left the room.

She stood for a long time, looking at the space where he had stood, wishing with all her heart that things could be different. That this Christmas she could ask for and receive the gift of Ethan in her life long after the holiday was over.

Leah killed as much time as she could before returning to her room. At the door, she paused and peered inside to see Ethan, his sister and their father clustered around Rebekah's bed. The little girl was sitting up and chattering excitedly. Charity saw Leah in the doorway and hurried over and took her arm.

"Guess what, Leah. Papa has given his permission for Ethan and me to stay for the party tonight. Isn't that wonderful?"

TEN

The party was set to start at six-thirty. Charity took Rebekah to the rec room in a wheelchair. Leah helped guide the child's IV pole alongside; although Rebekah's fever had broken, her doctor had not authorized her being taken off the antibiotic.

The rec room swarmed with kids who were decorating the tree from boxes of ornaments piled on the floor. Two orderlies, an intern, and Ethan were patiently stringing lights around the tree, while Molly supervised and nurses helped the children.

"I thought your shift was through for the day," Leah said, to Molly.

"It is, but I couldn't leave everyone to party

without me. I called my husband and told him I'd be late tonight." She clamped her hands over her ears. "Loud in here, isn't it?"

"All good parties are loud." Leah noticed Rebekah and Charity standing to one side, staring wide-eyed at the activity. With their odd clothing, they did look a little out of place.

"Ethan's gotten into the swing of things, hasn't he?" Molly asked.

Leah watched him scurrying up a ladder with a handful of lights, which he proceeded to loop carefully around the tree. Even though his clothing was as dated as his sisters', he somehow looked less out of place. "I'm glad their father let Ethan and Charity stay," Leah told Molly.

"When are they leaving?"

"Ethan said they were catching a nine o'clock van."

"The party should be over by then."

"Do you think Rebekah will go home soon?"

"Sure, as long as she continues to improve. Hospital stays are expensive. Doctors try to get patients out of here quickly."

Leah realized that since she wouldn't be released until her mother and Neil came to get her on Thursday, she'd have been a patient for more than a week. Her hospitalization was going to cost Neil a bundle. She wondered if he would resent her for spending so much of his money when he wasn't even her father.

"Of course, most people have insurance," Molly said. "But the Amish don't."

"They don't have *any* insurance?"

Molly shook her head. "They believe in taking care of their own. Rebekah's bills will be paid in full by the Amish community."

Leah remembered the times she and her mother had had no one to fall back on. Leah's mother had never wanted to accept charity, especially not from Grandma Hall. They had had to apply for food stamps once, and when she was old enough to understand the meaning of taking public assistance, she had felt ashamed about it and hadn't wanted anyone at school to know. "I'm glad the Amish take care of each other," she said. "It must be nice."

"You're going to miss them when they go, aren't you?"

Leah gave Molly a self-conscious glance. "The room will be lonely without someone to talk to. And after they leave, I'll never see them again." Just saying it gave Leah a jolt.

"You could still visit them sometime. Maybe this summer."

Leah wondered what life was like on an Amish farm in the summer. Ethan and Charity must work all day. And at night, there'd be no TV or even electricity by which to read a book. She sighed. "I don't think so. Sometimes I wonder why we even met. It seems so pointless."

"Sometimes things happen for a purpose we can't see until much later. Sometimes we never know why," Molly said. "Whoops!" she interrupted herself. "Someone needs my help." She darted off to untangle a small boy who had managed to wrap himself in a garland of tinsel.

Leah went over to Charity and Rebekah. "So what do you think of all this Christmas stuff, Rebekah?"

"She's confused," Charity admitted. "As am I. Why do you decorate trees?"

"To celebrate, I guess."

"Celebrate what?"

Leah fumbled for words. "It's just what people do this time of the year. They decorate for the holidays, give presents and eat turkey dinners and do family stuff."

"Just like us!" Rebekah exclaimed.

Charity glanced around at the frenzied activity in the room and shook her head. "Not like us at all."

"Listen, why don't we slip into the library where it's quieter," Leah suggested. "We'll come out when it's time for cookies and Christmas music. I think one of the doctors is dressing up as Santa Claus."

"Who?" Rebekah asked.

"I'll explain later." Leah hustled her into the library, with Charity following close behind. The room looked friendly and smelled like books. The closed door kept out most of the noise.

"Look, Charity," Rebekah said, holding up a colorful picture book from a nearby table. "What's this about?"

Leah watched Charity leaf through pages filled with photos of paintings of beautiful angels. "Angels?" she asked Leah with astonishment. "Is this what you English think angels look like?"

Leah stiffened at the words *you English*. She studied the renderings of golden-haired beings wearing long, flowing robes and expressions of rapture. "I guess so."

"Why are they wearing these bird wings?"

"Because angels can fly." Leah paused, suddenly unsure. "Can't they?"

"Angels are spirits. They come and go as they please," Charity said. "Only the cherubim and seraphim have wings."

Leah stared hard at the book. She'd always seen angels drawn as attractive people wearing wings. "They don't look like this?"

"A cherub is a fearsome creature with four sides and four faces that look like a man, a lion, an eagle and a bull. The cherubim's wings cover their hands, and when their wings beat the air, it sounds like thunder. They flash fire as bright as lightning."

Leah listened, openmouthed. What Charity had described sounded more like a monster. "You're kidding. How do you know this?"

"It's written in Holy Scripture, in the Book of Ezekiel."

"*All* angels look like this?"

"No. . . . Isaiah says the seraphim have six wings and they fly through the Temple of God, singing 'Holy, holy, holy.'"

"But aren't there other kinds of angels? You know, regular angels?"

Rebekah giggled. "You're funny, Leah."

Charity smiled too. "There is Michael, the

Archangel, the guardian of Israel. And he leads armies of angels in battle against the fallen angels of Lucifer."

"You mean they go to war against each other?" Leah had imagined that angels hung around old churches and looked pretty.

"Lucifer once led a great rebellion against God, and for his disloyalty he and all his angels were thrown out of heaven. Now Lucifer roams the earth seeking men's souls, leading people away from God, deceiving us and causing us great trouble."

Leah was astounded. "All this is in the Bible? I had no idea." She thumbed through the angel book again, trying to imagine this strange spirit world.

"You know, angels can assume human form if they wish. Perhaps that is why they have been drawn this way." Charity touched one of the pictures. "Angels are strong and powerful. They are immortal, but they do not have souls as we do. They do God's bidding, but they serve people too."

"Serve? Like how?"

"In the Psalms it says that God commands his angels to guard us in everything we do. And in the Book of Hebrews it says that we are to be charitable to strangers because we do not know when we might be entertaining angels."

Charity's knowledge about angels astounded Leah. And it intrigued her to think such possibilities existed. "So now I have to be nice to *everybody*?"

Charity giggled. "You sound as if kindness is a chore."

Leah blushed. "Well, there are people I know who *aren't* angels for sure. But you really believe angels exist, don't you?"

"Of course."

"Even though we can't see them?"

"We can see them if they allow us to, but even if we do meet one, we do not always know it. They can seem most ordinary."

"But why would one appear to a person?"

"Sometimes to help us if we are in trouble. Sometimes to fight off evil."

"Why don't they always come to people's rescue?" Leah wondered where the angels had been when her grandmother had been in such terrible pain and had lain dying.

"Sending an angel is God's choice."

Leah could tell by the expressions on the faces of the Amish girls that they believed everything they were saying. Personally, she thought the whole discussion was bizarre. To her, God seemed arbitrary and angels better imagined as the sweet-faced, winged creatures she saw in the books, rather than the frightening creatures Charity had first described.

The library door opened, and Molly poked her head inside. "Come on, you three. We're about to put the angel on top of the tree."

Out in the rec room, Leah stood against the wall with Charity, Rebekah and Ethan, but her mind was elsewhere. Charity's voice, her words and deep convictions, were impossible to forget.

An intern had climbed the ladder with the angel and was placing it on the topmost branch of the tree. The decorative angel was robed in a red-and-white velvet gown. Its hair was golden, and its wings of wire were overlaid with white gauze. The intern scrambled down the ladder and folded it hastily. Across the room someone flicked off the overhead lights.

"Are we ready?" Molly called.

A chorus of children's voices called, "Yes!"

Molly threw a switch, and hundreds of lights blazed to life on the tree. The onlookers clapped and cheered—all except for Leah and the three Amish beside her. In the beautiful glow of the Christmas lights, their faces looked troubled. Leah allowed her gaze to linger on the angel, which was bathed in pale yellow light from the bulbs on nearby branches.

She was positive that the others in the room thought the angel ornament was beautiful, perfect. But to Leah, the angel now looked waxy and fake. It was just a doll, bearing little resemblance to the heavenly creature it was supposed to represent.

ELEVEN

Leah didn't sleep well that night. She tossed and turned, remembering the party and her Amish friends' reactions to it. Rebekah had been frightened of the man dressed as Santa Claus and had taken the gift he offered only after Leah had taken it first and pressed it into her hand.

"May I have it?" Rebekah had asked Ethan, who had looked uncertain about the whole thing.

"I'm not sure you should take something from a stranger," he said.

"It's all right," Leah told them. "It won't be much. Probably a plastic toy or some candy."

Ethan nodded, and Rebekah carefully pulled

off the paper, her movements slow and deliberate—so different from the other kids, who were ripping paper and ribbon to shreds to get to their gifts. Inside hers was a plastic doll. "I like Rose better," Rebekah said solemnly, handing the doll to Leah.

"You can keep it," Leah said. "It's a present."

Rebekah shook her head. "No, thank you. She is not right for a plain person."

Later, Leah had asked Charity, "What could be so awful about taking a plastic doll?"

"We do not believe in collecting material things. Rebekah has a doll. Why does she need two?"

Eating cookies and cake and drinking punch were much more to their liking. They all loved sweets, and Ethan ventured a grin of approval when he bit into a powdery white butter cookie decorated like a snowman.

Charity whispered, "Oma makes wonderful gingerbread, but I like this very much. Maybe even better."

A nurse stepped forward with a guitar and invited the audience to join her in singing Christmas songs, including "Frosty, the Snowman," "Rudolph, the Red-Nosed Reindeer" and "Jingle Bells."

The Amish listened, and Leah tried to imagine what it must be like to hear these songs for the first time. When the nurse began to lead the group in singing carols, Leah glanced at Charity to see if she knew the words. Charity knew them well, and even Ethan and Rebekah sang along. Leah sang too, even though for her, the carols were simply a tradition of the season. For the Amish, singing the words had religious meaning.

When "Silent Night" was played, Charity sang softly in German. As the beautiful music played, Leah felt a lump rise in her throat, in spite of herself. The shimmering tree, the music and children's voices gave her goose bumps. When her gaze fell on the Christmas angel atop the tree, she deliberately glanced away.

After the party, Leah and Rebekah returned to their room and said goodbye to Charity and Ethan. This time Rebekah didn't cry at being left, but Leah felt pangs of regret. She caught Ethan's gaze, and their eyes held. For an instant she thought he might give her a farewell hug. But he didn't. She felt disappointment, although she hadn't really expected him to do something like that.

"Good night, Leah," he said softly.

"But you will come back?"

"On Monday."

"My biopsy—"

"I will be here when you wake up from your surgery."

"Do you promise?"

He touched her cheek. "Yes, I promise."

Long after they were gone and Rebekah slept, Leah lay awake, listening to the night sounds of the hospital. She wished she could sleep away the night and the whole next day. She wanted the biopsy to be over. She wanted Ethan to return.

She sighed and threw back the bedcovers. Perhaps a walk to the rec room would make her feel sleepy, or at least help pass the time.

The rec room was deserted. The aroma of the Christmas tree filled the room, and although its lights had been turned off, it still looked magnificent.

She stood in front of it, fingering the fragrant pine needles and remembering other trees and other Christmases. The tree comforted her. She imagined the woods it had come from. The tree too had been snatched from all that was familiar and thrust into a world that was completely foreign.

Behind her she heard the door open, and she turned to see a nurse silhouetted in the doorway. Leah squinted, then recognized her. "You're Gabriella," she said. "Rebekah talks about you. I've seen you in our room at night."

Gabriella's auburn hair was short with long fringy bangs, and her eyes were dark brown. "She is a precious child, but I've been looking for you."

"I'll bet you're doing bed checks and found mine empty. Sorry about that, but I couldn't sleep." Leah expected a lecture about being out of bed in the middle of the night.

"I knew where to find you."

"There's noplace else to go," Leah said with a heavy sigh.

"Where would you go if you could go anywhere?"

Leah paused, struck by the question. *Where would I go?* "I'm not sure."

"You're not unhappy here, are you?"

Leah thought about Rebekah, Charity and Ethan. "I'm not unhappy," she said.

"Come," Gabriella said, taking her hand. "You should go back to bed."

Obediently Leah followed her out of the rec room and down the hall. "What's bothering you? Why can't you sleep?" Gabriella asked.

"I—I think I'm worried about Monday," Leah confessed. Until that moment, she hadn't consciously been thinking about the biopsy at all.

Gabriella stopped, rested her hands on Leah's shoulders and looked deeply into her eyes. "Don't be afraid, Leah. Everything will work out for the best."

"But how do you know?"

"Things happen for a purpose. Even if we don't understand them."

Leah sighed. "You sound like Molly."

"Molly likes you very much."

"I like her too," Leah said. "She's nice. And she really cares about people."

"You remind her of someone."

"Who?"

"That's for Molly to tell you."

Curious, Leah started to question Gabriella, but the nurse took her hand and led her back to her room. Together they checked on Rebekah, who was sound asleep. The child's skin was cool, and Leah realized that Rebekah really was getting well.

Gabriella smoothed Leah's bedcovers and, reluctantly, Leah crawled between the sheets. "I'm still not sleepy," Leah insisted.

"Do you want me to stay with you until you fall asleep?"

Leah started to say *"I'm no baby,"* but stopped. "My grandma Hall is the only other person who's ever done that for me. But that was a long time ago."

Gabriella took her hand. "Then it's my turn now."

Leah found the woman's touch comforting, and soon a feeling of serenity and contentment stole over her. Her eyelids grew heavy. "Gabriella, why are the Amish so different?"

"It is their belief and their custom to be different."

The answer didn't satisfy Leah. "I like them, but I don't understand why they live the way they do."

"Sometimes simplicity is a good thing. It keeps people focused on what's important."

Leah yawned, and her thoughts turned again to her upcoming surgery. "Things will be all right with the biopsy, won't they?"

"God never puts more on a person than the person can bear."

Leah fell asleep and dreamed of Amish buggies, of men who looked like Ethan, and of huge pieces of medical equipment towering over her like birds of prey, intent on devouring her.

"Will you read to me from my book?"

Rebekah's question pulled Leah from her deep sleep. Sunlight spilled through the window, and her breakfast tray sat on her bedside table, the plate still covered by a stainless steel dome. She'd slept so soundly, she hadn't even heard it being delivered. She shook her head to clear it and struggled to a sitting position. "What time is it?"

Rebekah stood beside Leah's bed, her eyes level with the mattress. The IV line had been removed from the girl's hand, and a Band-Aid covered the place where the needle had been. Rebekah shrugged.

Still groggy, Leah smiled. "That late, huh? I'd better get moving."

"You were sleeping so long."

"Yeah. I guess I stayed up too late. Why didn't you wake me?"

"Because Gabriella said not to."

"You talked to Gabriella?"

Rebekah nodded and offered a bright smile. "She told me goodbye. She said I'd be going home tomorrow."

Leah felt jolted. Gabriella wouldn't have told Rebekah that unless it was true. *Going home.* And away from the world Leah was a part of.

TWELVE

Leah mumbled, "Well, I guess after you leave, Gabriella and Molly will be my only friends."

Rebekah looked stricken. "You will be lonely."

Leah tousled the child's hair. "Don't worry about it. My mom will be here Thursday." She got out of bed. "Let me freshen up and then I'll read to you."

Leah quickly showered and was putting on her makeup when Rebekah appeared in the bathroom doorway, shyly looking in. "May I watch?"

"Sure."

Rebekah had already dressed. She fluffed the

skirt of her dress and settled on the edge of the tub, where she studied Leah intently with saucer-wide eyes. "Why do you put paint on your face?"

Leah glanced down at her. "To look pretty."

"But you already look pretty."

"Well, thanks, but without mascara, my eyes disappear."

"They do?" The child sat up straighter, squinting to examine Leah's eyes more closely.

Bemused, Leah said, "I guess that doesn't make sense to you. Let's just say I put on makeup because it's my custom, like wearing that cap on your head is yours."

Rebekah seemed to accept this explanation, but when Leah turned the blow-dryer on her shoulder-length, precision-cut hair, Rebekah asked, "Why do you cut your hair off? The Bible says hair is a woman's glory."

"What does that mean?"

"I don't know."

Leah laughed. "I like my hair this way, and I think it looks best on me. I guess it's hard for us to understand each other's ways sometimes."

Rebekah nodded and changed the subject. "My sister Sarah got married in November. She married Israel Kramandam."

"That's nice. Did they go on a honeymoon?"

"What's a honeymoon?"

Leah realized that if the Amish didn't believe in mingling with the world, it was doubtful they would indulge in this particular custom. "A kind of vacation two people take when they get married," she explained.

Rebekah giggled. "Who would do their work? Who would feed the cows?"

"Sorry—I forgot about those cows. So, what do an Amish couple do when they get married?"

"They go around visiting people on other farms. They get to sleep over and get presents." Rebekah's face looked animated. "Then in the spring, they move into their own house. I liked Sarah's wedding. Everybody came."

"Who's everybody?"

"All the plain people. Mama said three hundred were coming and for Papa to fetch enough chairs because no one was going to say that Tillie Longacre didn't know how to put on a wedding feast," Rebekah said in an imitation of her mother's voice. "Mama and Oma cooked and cooked for weeks. I helped."

"Wow, that's a lot of people." Leah thought about her own mother's weddings. The last three ceremonies had been attended only by Leah and one or two of her mother's friends. "Was your sister's dress pretty?"

Rebekah's brow knitted as she considered the question. "All our dresses are plain."

"Didn't she wear a fancy wedding gown?"

Rebekah shrugged. "It was white. But not fancy."

"Were there flowers?"

Rebekah shook her head. Neil and Leah's mother's wedding had been small, but Leah's mother had worn an expensive dress of pale blue silk and carried an exquisite cascade of orchids and roses, and the ring Neil had slipped onto her finger had been huge and glittering. "I personally think your plain way is better," she said.

Leah's approval obviously pleased Rebekah. "When I grow up and get married, will you come to my wedding?"

"Could I come? I mean, since I'm not Amish?"

Rebekah pondered the question. "I'll ask Ethan. He knows everything."

The mention of Ethan made Leah's pulse quicken. "Well, you have to grow up first," she told Rebekah. "And by then, who knows where I'll be?" Rebekah looked as if she didn't understand, and Leah realized that for a girl whose family had lived in the same place for generations, the concept of moving from state to state, city to city, rented apartment to rented house wouldn't make any sense at all.

"Come on," Leah said, taking Rebekah's hand. "Let's go read your book, and I'll let you show me some more stories about angels. That way I'll be able to recognize one if I see it."

Rebekah giggled. "You can't see them, Leah."

Leah feigned exasperation. "Just my luck. So how am I supposed to believe in something I can't see?"

Still clinging to Leah's hand, Rebekah tilted her head upward. "Because you see them with your heart, not your eyes."

Leah nodded, saying nothing but wishing she had the same simple faith.

Leah found Sunday afternoon unbearably boring. She didn't want to watch TV, especially since Rebekah wasn't used to it. The rec room was too noisy and the video game room was full of kids waiting to play. Even the library offered no refuge. She was standing in the kitchen, ready to throw herself on the floor in frustration, when Molly walked in. "Rescue me!" Leah cried, grabbing the nurse by the shoulders.

"Bored, are we?" Molly asked with a laugh.

"Watching paint dry would be more exciting."

Molly glanced at her watch. "I'm filling in for a friend who's sick, but I don't have to sign on for another thirty minutes. Why don't you throw on some street clothes and I'll take you downstairs to the main cafeteria. Maybe the change of scenery will do you good."

Leah practically set a speed record dressing in jeans and a sweatshirt. She must have lost some weight—a quick check in the mirror revealed that her jeans looked baggy. But except for the plastic ID bracelet on her wrist, she didn't look like a patient at all.

"You know," she told Molly during the ride down in the elevator, "I'm going to be pretty miffed if they can't find anything wrong with me after I've wasted almost a whole week in the hospital."

"Is your knee still sore?"

"Yes." Leah rotated the kneecap and winced.

"And my back too. Maybe it's arthritis from waiting around this place for so long."

Molly chuckled. "I don't think so. By tomorrow night you'll have a diagnosis. Hang in there."

They entered the cafeteria, a spacious, carpeted room with banks of floor-to-ceiling windows. Outside, the weather looked raw and blustery, with flurries of snow swirling wildly. Leah shivered, missing the sun-drenched Texas weather.

"This place makes the best cake. They call it Chocolate Decadence and believe me, it *is*!" Molly said. "Want to try a piece?"

"Is that a trick question? You bet I do!"

Molly went to the dessert area of the food bar and returned with a plate of triple-layer chocolate cake studded with white chocolate chunks, slathered with chocolate icing and drizzled with dark chocolate syrup. She also carried an extra plate and two forks. The cake tasted so good, Leah savored each rich bite with a sigh.

"Feel better?" Molly asked.

"Much." Leah laid down her fork. "If I forget to tell you later, thanks for being so nice to me."

"You're easy to be nice to, Leah."

"You really make me feel like a person instead of a medical dilemma. The doctors make me feel like I'm some sort of puzzle to be solved."

"Doctors get so focused on a patient's symptoms and medical data that they sometimes lose sight of the human element. I guess that's where nurses come in. And I'm glad you feel that I'm your friend. For me, that's an important part of nursing."

Leah took another bite of cake. "I was thinking the other day about what it might be like to be a nurse. I mean, everyone has to do something for a job. Do you think I would make a good nurse?"

"It's hard work," Molly said. "And getting harder. I plan to go back to school in the summer just to learn more about certain diseases. Nursing isn't for the fainthearted, Leah."

"And maybe I'm not smart enough."

"If it was just memorizing medical information, anyone could go into nursing, but in order to be a good nurse, you must genuinely want to take care of sick people. I've been on different rotations all over this hospital, and I'm telling you, some people are real pills. They're demanding and cranky and you have to keep reminding yourself that they aren't purposely trying to make your life miserable."

Leah laughed. "Is that why you stick to the pedi floor? Because you're bigger and can make the kids do what you want?"

"How'd you guess?" Molly's eyes twinkled; then her face softened. "Actually, I'm on the pedi floor because I really like the kids and hate seeing them suffer. And"—she took a breath—"because of Emily."

"Who's Emily?"

"She was my sister."

"Was?"

"She died when she was just fourteen—more than twenty-five years ago. And I haven't gotten over it yet."

THIRTEEN

"**Y**our sister died? What happened to her?" Leah saw pain etched in Molly's face.

"It was leukemia. Back then we didn't have the drugs and chemotherapy protocols we have now. Bone marrow transplants were highly experimental too. Most kids who got the disease died."

Leah shuddered and thought of Grandma Hall. "How old were you when it happened?"

"Emily was diagnosed when I was eight and she was twelve, but I remember it like it was yesterday. My parents were beside themselves. And for a while, I was jealous of all the attention Emily was getting. But once I saw how sick the chemo made her, I got over being jealous."

"I never had a sister, but sometimes I wish I did."

"Well, Emily truly was a special girl. She was smart, pretty, popular, but not the least bit stuck-up. I adored her. When she got sick, she was in the hospital for weeks at a time. We lived on a farm, and the only hospital that had a children's oncology unit was three hundred miles away. Mom had to stay with Emily, and during the week Dad worked and stayed with me while I went to school.

"On the weekends, he and I would drive the three hundred miles to visit. I resented it at first, but one time when I got there, Emily was vomiting horribly and all her hair had fallen out from the medication. It was such a shock seeing her bald, I broke down crying and ran out of the room. Emily had had beautiful, long hair, and in less than a week it was totally gone."

Leah saw the mental picture all too clearly. "How did you decide to become a nurse?"

Molly pushed her cake plate aside and leaned back in her chair. "There was a nurse on the floor, an elderly woman, who would sit with my sister for hours when my mother had to get away and get some rest. She was so patient and kind. I'll never forget her. She knew the special patients, the really sick ones, by name. She called them her little angels. Every time Emily had to return to the hospital, Mrs. Duncan was there to take care of her."

"Did your sister have to go back to the hospital often?"

"Not at first. But when she was barely fourteen, she went out of remission, and then she was there almost all the time. The week she died, I stayed out of school. My dad had a neighbor look after the farm, and we all sat by Emily's bedside, watching her die."

Molly paused, and visions of Grandma Hall on her deathbed passed through Leah's head. "It was terrible," Molly said. "But Mrs. Duncan stayed with us the whole time. And at Emily's funeral, she took the day off and drove to our place for the service. I knew then that I wanted to be like that lady. I never considered being anything but a nurse."

Molly's story had touched Leah. "I'm really sorry about your sister. And I know what it's like to lose someone you love." She told Molly briefly about her grandmother's illness and death. "I know how much Ethan and his sisters believe in God, but I wonder why God lets these things happen."

"God doesn't owe us an explanation," Molly said. "But still, there's something comforting about faith. And it's hard *not* to believe in God when you live on a farm all your life. Every winter, all life seems to die. Yet every spring, life returns. Scientific explanations aside, it always seems miraculous to me."

Leah thought about Ethan and his family. Maybe their faith sprang partly from their sense of belonging to the land.

Molly looked at her watch. "I'm late for duty."

The two of them hurried back upstairs, Leah deep in thought. Maybe after this biopsy was complete and she was back on Neil's farm, she could think about making friends at her new high school. Maybe this new life in Indiana wouldn't be so bad after all.

If only my mother can just make this marriage work.

Leah was given a pill to help her sleep that night, and early the next morning a nurse gave her a shot to relax her before her surgery. The medicine worked; she was feeling very calm when an orderly arrived and rolled her on a gurney down the hall to the elevators and the surgical floor.

Once in the O.R. area, Leah was shifted to a gurney and hooked up to an IV line. Efficient nurses busied themselves with patients waiting in a line of hospital beds for one of the four operating rooms. Even though she was feeling relaxed, Leah wished at this moment that her mother could be there.

Dr. Thomas appeared. He wore a green surgical scrub suit and a green cap over his hair. "How're we doing?" he asked.

"A little scared," Leah mumbled.

His eyes crinkled at the corners. "Well, once the anesthesiologist gets hold of you, you'll sleep through the whole thing." He patted her shoulder.

The anesthesiologist talked to her briefly, then slipped a needle into her IV line. "This is going to make you sleepy," he said.

He left, and Molly's face peered down at her. "Hi."

Leah managed a smile of gratitude. "You came to see me."

"I couldn't let you go in there without telling you good luck."

"Will you be here when I wake up?"

"No. They'll take you into recovery, and once you're fully awake, you'll be brought back to the floor. I'll see you there."

Leah reached for Molly's hand, and as the medication spread, making her feel weightless and numb, she mouthed, "Thank you." The last thing she saw was Molly's smiling face and, over Molly's shoulder, the face of Gabriella. Leah wanted to thank the other nurse for coming too, but the drug was making her so drowsy, she couldn't. Gabriella blew her a kiss, and then a curtain of darkness descended over Leah.

She regained consciousness in another room, where other patients were also awakening from operations. Nurses took her blood pressure every fifteen minutes and offered her sips of water. Her knee was sore and bandaged, and her finger had been rebandaged. Had the doctor taken a sample of that bone for the biopsy too? In no time she felt clearheaded, and an orderly took her back to the pediatric floor.

As the orderly rolled Leah's bed into place,

Rebekah cried, "You're back! Oh, Leah, you're back."

Leah said, "I slept through the whole thing." Her throat was sore, and when Molly came to welcome her, she explained, "That's from the tube they put down your throat during surgery. It'll clear up in a day or two."

"Have you heard anything about what's wrong with me?" Leah asked.

"No. They'll call your mother and talk to her about it."

"Why? I'm the one going through this. My mother's halfway around the world. Don't I have any rights?"

"You have lots of rights. It'll be up to your doctor. He'll decide how much to tell you. And I know Dr. Thomas. He's pretty straightforward with his patients." Molly gestured to a vase of beautiful flowers sitting on Leah's bedside table. "These were delivered while you were having your biopsy."

"Who sent them?" Molly handed her the card. It read: *We're thinking of you. Recover quickly. Call you later. Love, Mom and Neil.* Leah was pleased, and also a little embarrassed about her outburst. She peered up at Molly. "I guess they didn't forget what was happening today."

"I guess not," Molly said with a grin. "I hear the lunch trays, so I've got to run. I'll check in with you before my shift ends."

Rebekah sidled over to Leah's bed. "Are you all right, Leah?"

Leah scooted up in the bed, putting on a cheerful expression for the child. "Just fine. See?" She pulled back the covers and showed Rebekah her bandage-wrapped knee. "The doctor took a tiny chip of my bone and sent it to the lab to be examined."

"Why?"

"To see why it's sore. To see why my finger broke for no reason."

"My oma has rheumatism," Rebekah said. "Mama fixes her some tea to make it stop hurting." Her face brightened. "Maybe she can make some tea for you."

"Maybe."

The door swung open. Expecting the lunch trays, Leah turned. But the doorway was filled with Ethan. Rebekah ran to him.

Leah's mouth went dry and her heart hammered. He had come, just as he had promised.

FOURTEEN

"Hello, Leah." Ethan scooped Rebekah up in his arms and approached Leah's bed.

"Hi." She realized that she didn't have a bit of makeup on, not even lipstick.

"Your biopsy went well?"

"I did fine, but I don't know anything yet—"

"Where's Mama?" Rebekah interrupted.

"Mama's home, fixing you a welcome-back dinner. Papa's downstairs signing you out. You're coming home."

"Gabriella already told me."

Leah's heart sank. She was glad for Rebekah, but she was going to miss all of them.

"Did Charity come with you?" she asked. "I wanted to tell her goodbye."

"She is here. She dislikes the elevator and is walking the stairs."

Charity entered the room, flushed from the climb, her eyes sparkling. After hugging her sister, she asked Leah about her surgery.

"Help me, Charity," Rebekah said. She'd gone to the closet and dragged out a small duffel bag.

Minutes later Mr. Longacre arrived. Not wanting to be in the way while they packed up the child's few belongings, Leah eased out of bed and into the hall, using a pair of crutches. Her knee was sore, but she hobbled down to the rec room. It was crowded with children.

Leah let herself into the library, which was empty. She sank into a chair and stared at the floor. Her days and nights in the hospital stretched before her like a ribbon of lonesome country highway. Her mother and Neil wouldn't be arriving for three more days.

When she heard the door open, she willed the intruder to go away. She wasn't in the mood to be disturbed.

"Leah?"

She turned to see Charity. "Are you all leaving now?"

Charity nodded. "Rebekah wants to say goodbye. And so do I."

"Goodbye," Leah said. She started to say, "Tell Rebekah I'll call her," then remembered that they didn't have a phone. She sighed. "All right, I'll be back to the room in a minute."

Charity stepped forward. "I'm glad you are alone, because I want to give you something." She thrust out a small package wrapped in brown paper and tied with twine.

"What's this?"

"A gift. For Christmas. I made it for you."

Instantly Leah felt ashamed. She'd been feeling sorry for herself and hadn't given a thought to a present for anyone. "I—I don't know what to say."

"I hope you like it."

"Can I open it now?"

"If you wish to."

Leah heard eagerness in Charity's voice. She tugged at the string and pulled away the paper. Inside lay a piece of linen cloth, and on it, etched in meticulous tiny pink and green cross-stitches, was a cascade of small blossoms surrounded by leaves. Her name, LEAH, was stitched in the center. "It's so beautiful! Thank you."

"Do you really like it? It's a covering for a pillow for your bed. I hope every time you look at it, you will think of me."

Leah didn't know how to sew, but she knew fine stitching when she saw it. The threads were even and delicate, and the image of Charity working so diligently to create the gift brought a lump to Leah's throat. "I won't forget you," she said. "You're a real friend, and your gift is wonderful."

"Plain people are not supposed to feel prideful, but I feel much pride. Perhaps God will forgive me for this small sin," Charity confided shyly.

Leah stood and hugged her. "I'll put this on my bed as soon as I get home."

"Before we return to the room, Ethan wants to talk to you," Charity said.

Leah felt her heart almost stop. "Ethan's with you?"

"Right outside the door. I told him I would make an excuse to Papa so that he could have some time alone with you."

"Your father wouldn't approve, would he? He wouldn't want Ethan to be alone with an

English girl. I don't want the two of you to get into trouble."

Charity retreated to the door and with a mischievous grin said, "Sometimes it is easier to get forgiveness than permission."

When Ethan came into the room, Leah felt her mouth go dry. He was so tall, and his serious blue-eyed gaze turned her knees to jelly. She had long since gotten over his old-fashioned way of dressing. The shapeless, unstylish dark fabric covered the gentlest person she had ever known. He walked over and stood looking down at her. "I will be leaving soon, Leah."

"Then I guess this is goodbye forever."

"You cannot say that, for no one can see into tomorrow."

She squared her jaw. "If you weren't Amish, I could phone you. I could drive to your house and you could come to mine. I could meet you at a mall. We could go to a movie together. I could ask you to a dance at my school."

"But I *am* Amish."

Leah fought back tears as she grasped the impossibility of their situation. "Are you going to take Martha Dewberry for another ride in your buggy?" She pictured a warm summer night under countless stars. And Ethan in the moonlight with another girl. An Amish girl.

Gently he ran his fingers along the side of her face. "There is only one girl I want to take in my buggy. It is not Martha."

"Are you just saying that to make me feel better, Ethan?"

"I told you, Leah Lewis-Hall—I do not lie."

"Have you ever kissed her, Ethan? Have you kissed any girl?" Leah's voice was barely audible, and she was trembling. Her heartbeat quickened.

Mutely he shook his head.

She whispered, "Will you kiss me?" She wanted to be his first kiss. Her mother once told her that the first kiss was the one a person never forgot. She wanted Ethan to remember her for all time. "For hello and goodbye at the same time," she added.

He lifted her chin with his forefinger and very slowly lowered his head until his mouth was only inches away. His breath smelled like cinnamon and felt warm on her skin. Gently he pressed his lips to hers, and she closed her eyes and sank into the velvet softness of it. Leah had been kissed before, but she knew that this kiss,

Ethan's kiss, was the one that would matter to her for the rest of her life.

When he ended the kiss, when he stepped back, she saw that he looked shaken. She hoped he didn't feel guilty about kissing her. "I— I . . ." She fumbled for words.

He placed the tips of his fingers against her mouth. "Your lips are lovely, Leah. Worth waiting for." He took a deep breath. "My father may come looking for me. We should return to the room."

"If I leave with you," Leah said, "he'll see what has happened between us on my face. I can't hide it."

Ethan nodded. "Then you return to the room and I will go straight down to the lobby."

She cast him one last lingering look and hurried from the room as quickly as her sore knee would allow. Pausing outside the door, she fought to regain her composure.

Rebekah sprang toward her like an overeager puppy when Leah stepped into their room. "I've been waiting for you to come! I couldn't go without saying goodbye." Rebekah flung her arms around Leah's waist. "I miss you already."

"I'll miss you, too. You were the best room-mate in the whole world."

"Papa has taken Rebekah's things down to the lobby," Charity said, her gaze sweeping Leah knowingly. "The bus is leaving soon. Ethan?"

"He went straight downstairs."

Charity nodded and took Rebekah's hand. "Then we must go now."

Leah felt a wave of panic. How could she let them leave her? "Can I write you?" she asked suddenly. "Does the mailman deliver to the Amish?"

Charity broke into a smile. "Of course." She grabbed a pencil and jotted down her address. "Write me—us," she corrected. "If you wish to write to my brother, enclose it in a letter to me and I will make certain that Ethan gets it. I will be praying for you, Leah. I will pray that your tests come out well."

Leah watched the door swing shut behind Charity and Rebekah. The silence in the room made her feel depressed and anxious. It wasn't her tests that worried her. It was losing her friends that was breaking her heart. It was losing Ethan because they came from two differ-ent worlds. No amount of wishing could change things. Amish and English simply didn't mix. Leah realized that it was almost a miracle that they had gotten to meet and become friends at all.

Leah sat at the table in her room, her dinner tray in front of her, toying with the food. She heard a light knock and sat up. Her door opened and Dr. Thomas entered.

The look on his face told her that he had news he didn't want to deliver. She set down her fork. "What is it?"

He pulled a chair closer to hers. "I believe I have a diagnosis for you."

"And?"

"And based on the results of your bone scan, you have osteogenic sarcoma. Bone cancer."

FIFTEEN

Leah thought she was having a bad dream. "Bone cancer? There must be a mistake."

Dr. Thomas took her hand. She pulled away, not wanting this man to comfort her when he was shattering her world. "Osteogenic sarcoma is a disease that hits teens and people in their early twenties," he told her. "It often starts in the leg bones, the femur and tibia. It's unusual for it to be present in the kneecap or finger. A tumor has grown on the inside of your finger and weakened the bone. That's why it broke. Another tumor is growing under your kneecap."

"I don't believe it."

"I wouldn't make it up, Leah."

"So *if* it's true, what are you going to do about it?"

"We'll fight aggressively," he said. "Chemotherapy is part of the standard treatment."

She recalled the cancer patients on the pedi floor; children bald from chemo, hooked to IVs. And Grandma Hall. This couldn't happen to her. "I don't want chemo."

"Leah, your life is at stake."

"I want to talk to my mother." The words surprised her.

Dr. Thomas nodded. "I have a call in to her. When she calls back, I'll send for you. I'll put all of us on my speakerphone and we'll have a three-way conversation."

Leah's eyes stung from holding back tears. "Can I be by myself now? I have to think about what you've told me."

The doctor stood. His hand rested on her shoulder. "Leah, I know this is a blow, but you can lick it. I promise to help you every step of the way."

Long after he was gone, she sat at the table, numbly staring into space. Somewhere down the hall, someone was playing Christmas music. How could she feel joy and peace when she'd been told she had cancer?

She sighed, and a long, shuddering sob escaped. Leah clenched her fists together. *I won't cry,* she told herself. Crying would make the whole thing real. Crying would mean acceptance, and she wasn't ready for that.

Leah felt like a caged animal. She wanted to tell someone. She wanted to call a friend and talk. Except that she had no friends. Charity and Ethan were on their way home, and even when they got there, Leah couldn't call them. She could write them a letter, but by the time they got it, the news would be old. And besides, it wasn't as if they could drive back to Indianapolis to console her.

Her door opened, and Molly came hesitantly into the room. Her expression told Leah she'd heard the news. "Leah . . . honey . . . I'm so sorry."

"Maybe he's wrong," Leah said. "Doctors can be wrong, can't they?"

"They can." Molly paused, then added, "But I don't think he'd have told you what he did if he wasn't sure."

Leah drooped. "Why is this happening to me, Molly?"

"I don't know why. But I do know that you

have a wonderful doctor to help you through
it."

"But I don't want to go through it."

"Leah, chemo treatments aren't like they
used to be." Molly seemed to know that it was
the chemo, not the cancer, that was scaring
Leah the most.

"But he could be wrong," Leah insisted.

Molly didn't answer. Instead she put her
arms around Leah, and together they stood
while the joyous strains of Christmas music
danced in the air around them.

Eventually dinner trays were cleared away.
For the first time since she had checked into
the hospital, Leah turned on the TV set in her
room—mostly to keep herself distracted.

The room was lonely. She missed Rebekah
and Charity. Most of all, she missed Ethan. She
flipped through the TV channels aimlessly.

A night nurse brought her a pill. Leah asked,
"What's this?" She was half afraid it was some
form of chemotherapy.

"A sleeping pill," the nurse said. "Dr.
Thomas thought you might need it tonight."

"Do you know if Gabriella's come on duty
yet?"

"Who?"

"Gabriella. I don't know her last name, but she works on this floor at night."

The nurse shrugged. "Sorry. I don't know her, but I'm rather new to the nursing staff. If I run into anyone with that name, I'll send her straight to your room."

Leah swallowed the pill and waited for it to take effect. Much later during the night, she was vaguely aware that someone had come into her room. She struggled to talk, but she was too drowsy. She felt the squeezing band of the blood pressure cuff and the cool metal of the stethoscope against the inside of her arm.

"Gabriella?" she whispered.

No answer.

Leah fell back into a deep and dreamless sleep.

"Leah, wake up!"

Someone was shaking her. "Go away."

"It's six A.M. Dr. Thomas sent me. I'm supposed to bring you to his office. Your mother's on the phone, and she wants to talk to you."

Leah struggled to throw off the grogginess from the sleeping pill. The nurse helped her up, settled her into a wheelchair and headed down the hall. Leah grabbed a carton of orange juice at the nurses' station and sipped it during the ride up in the elevator. By the time she arrived at Dr. Thomas's office on the top floor, she was fully awake.

His office was small and cramped, and he was sitting behind a desk heaped with medical books and file folders. The nurse put on the chair's brake and left. Leah heard her mother's voice through the speaker phone. "This is preposterous," she was saying. "My daughter checks into your hospital less than a week ago with a broken finger, you diddle around with all kinds of testing and then you call and tell me she has *bone cancer*!"

"Mrs. Dutton, please listen—"

"No! You listen. I want to talk to Leah. Now."

Dr. Thomas looked at Leah.

She leaned forward. "I'm here, Mom."

"Oh, darling, are you all right?"

"Not really."

"You just sit tight, baby. I'm coming home just as soon as I can get packed up. Neil's making arrangements to get our tickets changed even as we speak."

The calendar on Dr. Thomas's desk showed

that it was Tuesday, December 21. It was late Tuesday in Japan. If everything went like clockwork, the soonest her mother and Neil could be there would be the next night. "Please get me out of here," Leah said. "Please don't make me spend Christmas in this place."

"Not to worry, Leah. We'll get you out of there as soon as possible—"

"Mrs. Dutton." Dr. Thomas cut in. "Now that we know what we're dealing with, we should get Leah started on chemo immediately."

"You do *not* have my permission to do *anything* to my daughter before I get there," her mother said sharply.

"I don't recommend waiting."

"I want a second opinion," Leah's mother said stubbornly.

"All the opinions in the world won't change the diagnosis, Mrs. Dutton."

Leah swallowed. The doctor wasn't backing down, but neither was her mother. At that moment, Leah was glad her mother was so strong-willed.

"I stand by my original statement," Leah's mother said. "Don't do anything to my daughter except take care of her daily needs until I get there. Is that clear, Dr. Thomas?"

"Perfectly." The doctor didn't look pleased. "I'll let you sign off with Leah."

"Mom . . . I sure wish you were here."

"I will be soon, Leah. You just hold on until Neil and I get there. We're not going to give up without a fight. You can count on it."

SIXTEEN

Leah felt immensely relieved after the conversation with her mother. Dr. Thomas still insisted that she had bone cancer. But at least Leah didn't feel so alone anymore. Just knowing that her mother was hurrying to be with her brought her comfort.

Now all I have to do is kill time until Mom arrives.

She hobbled to the rec room, using her crutches, and discovered that it was full of kids. She could barely stand to look at the ones who were obviously on chemotherapy. Their bald heads and gaunt bodies made her queasy with dread. This might be how she would look in a few months.

Leah ended up in front of the Christmas tree. The clean pine scent blocked out the medicinal odors of the hospital. She thought back to when Ethan had strung the lights in the tree's branches.

She gazed at the elaborately dressed angel ornament and thought over the strange things Charity had told her about angels. Nothing was the way it seemed. Leah had thought angels were just pretty inventions by the creators of fairy tales. Now she half believed they might be real. She had thought that her broken finger and sore knee were no big deal, but she'd been told she had bone cancer. She had thought Ethan and his sisters were backward and strange. Now she thought of them as dear friends whom she would remember as long as she lived. Nothing was ever the way it seemed.

Carefully she broke off a small twig from the towering tree. She wanted to take it back to her room and place it under her pillow so that she could smell its aroma and imagine the snowy woods on Ethan's farm. Maybe by touching and smelling the pine needles, she could imagine herself closer to Ethan and the things that he loved.

She went to the library, picked up a copy of

the Bible and returned to her room, curious to read about angels for herself. She read several stories, but she could not get a clear picture of these strange, heavenly beings. Sometimes they appeared as ordinary people. In other places they were "bright lights," striking fear and awe in people.

Molly stuck her head in the doorway. "Feel like a visitor?"

Leah smiled. "If it's you."

"It's me." Molly came inside and pulled out a chair at the table where Leah was sitting. "You reading the Bible?"

"I figured it couldn't hurt. Charity and Ethan made me curious."

Molly nodded. "Are you feeling better today?"

"As good as a person can feel after she's been told she has cancer."

"It's a bad blow, Leah."

"Yeah. Just think, when people ask what I got for Christmas, I can say, 'Bone cancer, how about you?' "

Molly made a face at Leah's black humor, then said, "Don't forget. I'll be your nurse if you stay in this hospital."

"I appreciate that." Leah remembered their

conversation about the nurse who had taken care of Molly's sister. "You'll be my Mrs. Duncan, won't you?"

"Yes. Except your case will have a better outcome than Emily's and your grandmother's. All cancer isn't fatal, you know. Many people can be cured. Or at least have long periods of remission."

Leah wasn't comforted. "If I do have bone cancer and I have to have chemo, what will it be like?"

Molly took a few minutes before answering. When she spoke, her words sounded as though they were coming from a medical text. "You'll be put on a protocol of drugs that will take from nine months to a year to administer. Most of the chemo is toxic—it kills cancer cells and normal cells. Your immune system will be weakened, so you'll have to be very careful about germs. Even a common cold can land you in the hospital.

"They'll probably want to surgically insert a catheter—a plastic tube—into your chest, for administering the chemo. That way they won't have to stick you with needles for every dose. No swimming and no contact sports while you're wearing the device because you might get an infection."

Leah grimaced, hating the idea of a tube protruding from her chest. "Will I throw up?"

"Sometimes. Some of the drugs are stronger than others. You can experience everything from mild nausea to vomiting."

Hearing all of this made Leah lightheaded. "Will my hair fall out?"

"Yes. You can wear a wig until it grows back. And it *will* grow back, Leah. The hospital sponsors seminars for cancer patients to help them cope. And to help them look good and feel better about themselves throughout their treatments. You'll learn makeup tricks and get clothing tips."

"Whoopee," Leah said without enthusiasm.

Molly smiled. "Any other questions?"

"Not right now. I think I know more than I want to know."

Molly leaned forward. "I have a question for you."

"Sure, ask me anything."

"Tell me about Gabriella."

Leah was caught off guard. "What about her? I mean, she's your friend, isn't she?"

Molly shook her head. "I don't know her."

"Are you serious? She's on the night shift. I thought you knew her."

Molly's expression looked guarded. "I know everybody on every shift. There's no Gabriella on our staff."

"But I've talked to her. She came into my room at night. Actually, she visited Rebekah first, and then she started talking to me when Rebekah was leaving."

"This troubles me, Leah. I've never met the woman and there's no record of her in our personnel files."

A creepy sensation inched up Leah's spine. "That's weird."

"Very weird," Molly agreed. "Listen, you need to alert us if it happens again. Push your call button no matter what time of day or night."

Leah frowned. "But she's been really nice to me. She would sit by Rebekah's bed all night when she was scared."

"Nurses haven't got time to sit by a patient's bed all night. The night-shift staff is minimal, and there's plenty of work to do."

"But why would she do it?" Leah watched Molly's face as she considered the question, as if deciding how much she should say.

"I don't want to frighten you."

"Too late."

Molly leaned forward. "There are some strange people in the world, and most of the time they're harmless. Some of them like to hang around hospitals. Fantasize about being nurses and doctors. Goodness knows why—there's nothing very glamorous about our jobs.

"Anyway, these people sometimes sneak into hospitals and pretend to be part of our community. Once we had a woman who haunted the neonatal ward—where the newborns are. She would sneak in and try to hold the babies. We tightened security and caught her. She went to a psychiatric hospital."

"And you think this Gabriella is some kind of a nutcase too?"

"I don't know what to think. But you and Rebekah are the only people who've seen her, and since Rebekah's gone, she may come back and visit you again."

"She already has."

"What!" Molly sat bolt upright. "When?"

"The night Rebekah left. I ran into Gabriella in the rec room. She walked me back to my room and stayed with me until I fell asleep."

Grim-faced, Molly shook her head. "I'm

having security beefed up. What does she look like?"

Leah closed her eyes to get a clearer picture of Gabriella. "She's pretty. Her hair's short and reddish. I think her eyes are brown. She's about your height and size." She opened her eyes and saw Molly's worried expression. "I don't think she'd harm anybody, Molly."

"Probably not," Molly said slowly. "Still, she doesn't belong up here. I don't like the idea of anyone sneaking in at night and bothering our patients."

"Well, if she shows up again, I'll push my call button."

"Good. Now, let me go and have a talk with security." Molly stood, told Leah not to worry and left.

Leah shuddered. What a crummy day this had turned out to be! She'd learned about the horrors of chemo and about a weirdo stalking the halls at night. A weirdo only *she* could identify.

Still, try as she might, Leah couldn't picture Gabriella doing anything mean, and she didn't want her to be turned in to security. "You'd better not come and see me again, Gabriella," she muttered under her breath. Then she clicked on the TV and turned the volume up to chase away the chills she felt.

Leah spent most of the next day reading, playing video games and watching TV. She wanted to keep her mind as busy as possible. When her mind did veer to the subject of cancer, she quickly shut out the frightening thoughts and grabbed something else to do.

After dinner, as she was settling down for the night, she heard a commotion in the hallway. Moments later her door swung open and there stood her mother—her face flushed from the icy December air—wearing a long fur coat and a look of steely determination.

SEVENTEEN

Leah threw her arms around her mother, hardly believing how much she'd missed her.

"Honey, we got here as soon as we could. Neil had to move heaven and earth to change our tickets so close to the holidays, but he did it."

Neil stood behind Leah's mother, looking tired but triumphant. Snowflakes clung to his head of silver-white hair, and his blue eyes were full of concern. "How are you, Leah?"

She was surprised to find she was glad to see him too. "I'm better now that the two of you are here," she told him.

Her mother squirmed out of her coat and

flopped into a chair. "We're exhausted. We flew from Japan to Los Angeles, then from L.A. to Chicago, but that's as far as we got. All air traffic was grounded in Chicago because of the weather. So Neil rented a car and we drove the last two hundred miles in a snowstorm."

"Thank you," Leah said to Neil.

"We're family," he said with a grin.

"How was Japan?" Leah felt obligated to ask. Now that the preliminary greetings were over, she felt awkward and overwhelmed.

"Japan was wonderful. We'll have lots of pictures to show you, but this isn't the time to talk about it." Roberta glanced at her husband and said, "Neil, be a dear and see if you can find us a hotel near the hospital. I need a hot bath and a good night's sleep."

"Are you hungry?" he asked.

"Order us a pizza." She turned to Leah. "I've eaten so much fish lately, I'm about to grow fins."

Neil left, and Roberta climbed up on Leah's bed and hugged her again. "It's *so* good to be back in the good old U.S.A. I thought I was too old to get homesick, but when I passed through customs in Los Angeles and that customs agent stamped my passport and said 'Welcome home,' I got all teary-eyed."

Leah allowed her mother to unwind, knowing that she'd get a chance soon enough to tell her what had happened in the hospital. She was glad of the distraction. She wasn't sure what she was going to say, or how much she wanted to tell her mother about the past week.

Her mother picked up Leah's bandaged hand. "So, this is what caused all the trouble?"

"And this." Leah tossed back the covers to expose her knee, still wrapped.

"I find it hard to believe. Honestly, you've been the picture of health all your life."

"Dr. Thomas said that this kind of cancer mostly hits teenagers."

"I still think we should get a second opinion. Neil thinks so too."

"If . . . If it's true," Leah said hesitantly, "then I want to stay in this hospital."

"Whatever for?"

"I know the nurses. I made some friends."

Her mother sighed and rubbed her temples. "We'll have to talk about it tomorrow. I'm too tired to think straight right now. But I will tell you one thing. If this Dr. Thomas doesn't impress me, you'll be out of here in the blink of an eye."

"I'm quite sure of my diagnosis, Mrs. Dutton."

Leah heard Dr. Thomas, but she kept her gaze on her mother. They were seated in his office, and her mother was regarding him warily.

"It's simply hard for me to believe, that's all," her mother said. "I mean, *cancer*."

Dr. Thomas picked up a stack of large gray envelopes. "Let me show you and Leah something."

He stood, turned and flipped a switch, and a light board attached to his wall glowed with fluorescent light. He extracted a piece of X-ray film from each envelope and snapped each one to the board. "Come closer."

Leah moved forward with her mother and saw a series of grayish white bones, from a skull all the way to bones in the feet. "Is that me?" she asked, fascinated.

"Yes. This is your skeleton, top to bottom, from your bone scan."

Leah was impressed and a bit freaked out. It was strange seeing herself without skin.

"So where's the problem?" her mother asked.

"Here," Dr. Thomas said, drawing a circle around Leah's right kneecap with a marking pen. "And here." He drew another circle around her left forefinger.

Leah squinted and saw that both areas looked dark, like small holes.

"Remember," the doctor said, "bones are dense and show up white on X-ray film. Dark space is the absence of bone."

"So?" Leah's mother asked.

"These dark areas indicate that the bone has been eaten away. This is very typical of bone cancer."

"But a few X rays can't tell the whole story," her mother argued.

"True, but based on these, I did the biopsy."

"And what did that say?"

"Here's the pathologist's report." He picked up a file and handed it to Leah's mother. "It's inconclusive, unfortunately. But based on years of treating this disease, I think Leah has osteo-genic sarcoma."

As he spoke, Leah began to feel icy cold.

"You *think*?" her mother retorted. "This is just your opinion?"

Dr. Thomas sighed. "My opinion counts, Mrs. Dutton. I'm a specialist who's treated many cases of this disease."

"All right, all right. If this is true, how do you treat it?"

Leah knew the answer already.

Dr. Thomas didn't answer immediately. Instead he laced his fingers together and leaned forward. "Long-term treatment, chemotherapy."

"Long-term? What about the short term?"

"Sometimes drastic measures are needed to preserve a person's life."

Leah felt a tingling sensation all through her body. He was leading up to something horrific. She could sense it. "Like what?" she asked, her heart pounding.

"Like removal of the appendage with the tumors."

"Y-You mean, removing the tumors," she clarified.

"No. I mean amputating your leg and finger."

"No way!" Her mother exploded off her chair. "Leah's a young woman with her whole life ahead of her. You cannot cut off her leg! I won't let you."

Dr. Thomas shook his head sadly. "Mrs. Dutton, I don't like telling you this either, but this *is* the only way to maximize her recovery. After the amputations, she'll undergo chemo. Once she goes into remission, we'll monitor her closely. The cure rate—"

Leah stopped listening. She was numb. She tried to imagine her leg gone, her finger missing, a tube in her chest, needles and medicine. She began to cry.

Instantly her mother was at her side. "Oh, honey, it'll be all right."

Leah couldn't talk. It would *never* be all right.

"There are prostheses now that look very lifelike," Dr. Thomas was saying. "You'll go through rehabilitation. We'll work with you."

"I don't want you to cut off my leg!" Leah shouted. "I want you to leave me alone!" She pushed herself out of the wheelchair and limped out of his office as quickly as her aching leg allowed her to move.

EIGHTEEN

Leah lay in bed, facing the wall, refusing to eat or talk to anyone who came to see her. Not even Molly could raise her spirits. "I'm supposed to be off for a week starting tomorrow," Molly said. "But I don't want to go away and leave you like this." When Leah didn't respond, Molly squeezed her shoulder and added, "You have friends to help you through this."

Her mother paced the floor, muttering under her breath, sometimes stopping by the bed and saying, "We don't have to take his word for this, Leah. I know X-ray technicians can do sloppy work. And the pathologist's report isn't even conclusive."

Leah let her mother voice all the anger and

frustration she was feeling. But she still had to face her own fear alone.

"I want to go home for Christmas," Leah said, the first words she'd spoken in hours.

"Don't you worry. There's no way I'd keep you here for the holidays."

"Then after Christmas—" Leah's voice broke.

"We're not going to think about that now."

"When are we going to think about it?"

Her mother leaned over Leah's bed and stared into her eyes. "You know, Leah, for a long time I had to do things I didn't want to do, just for the two of us to survive. I worked jobs I hated, left you with day care centers when I wanted to stay home with you. I even married men I didn't honestly love so that you and I could have a better life.

"I really love Neil and he really cares about us. He's the father you *should* have had all these years." Leah winced at the mention of her father. Her mother continued. "But that's not what I want to say. What I want to say is I'm not ready to give up this fight. Everything I have, I got because I fought for it."

Confused, Leah asked, "What are you talking about?"

"I'm going to make Dr. Thomas run that bone scan test again before we check out."

"And the biopsy?"

"We may do that again too, after the holidays, of course. I can't explain why I have a bad feeling about that test, but I do."

The fervor in her mother's voice lit a candle of hope inside Leah. "Do you really think the tests are wrong? Grandma Hall's tests weren't wrong."

Her mother shrugged. "I don't know what to think. All I know is that I would never forgive myself if I let them cut off your leg when I have this gnawing doubt inside me." She looked away for a moment, and Leah was shocked to see tears in her mother's eyes. Her mother never cried in front of her. "I have some regrets about the way I treated you and your grandmother, Leah."

"What regrets?" Leah had not heard her mother discuss her grandmother since the day of her funeral.

"I should have been kinder to her. She truly loved you, and I kept her out of your life for far too long."

Leah felt tears brimming in her own eyes.

"Why did you? I loved her too. And I only got to be with her when she was dying."

Her mother sniffed and hung her head. "I was bitter about your father leaving us. He wasn't well, you know. I mean psychologically. He couldn't handle the responsibilities of marriage and a family, so he left. I took it out on your grandmother because I couldn't get even with him. That was wrong of me. Then, once he died, my anger seemed so pointless."

Shocked by her mother's confession, Leah stared. Her mother was asking her to forgive her for her past mistakes. "Is that why you want Dr. Thomas to run the tests again? So you won't make another mistake?"

Her mother smiled ruefully, hugged Leah with startling strength, and then straightened. "I owe it to you. And I owe it to her too. Now, if you'll excuse me, I've got to corner Dr. Thomas."

Dr. Thomas agreed to redo the bone scan, as Leah's mother told her with a great deal of satisfaction. The test was scheduled for the following morning. Afterward, Leah would be checked out and sent home for Christmas. Once the holidays were over she would return to the hospital for reevaluation by a second bone specialist. Although she didn't want to spend another night in the hospital, Leah very much wanted the test run again.

Late in the afternoon, sensing that her mother was emotionally wrung out, Leah insisted that she and Neil go back to the hotel. "Come back in the morning," Leah told them. "I feel better about everything now. And I have plenty of stuff to do to keep busy."

"Are you sure? I will admit that jet lag is catching up with me."

"I'm sure," Leah said, waving them out the door.

Neil gave her a grateful look.

Once they were gone, though, Leah felt lonelier than ever. When she heard a knock on her door an hour later, she eagerly called, "It's open!"

The door opened a crack, and Ethan's voice said, "Leah?"

Her heart almost stopped. He was the last person she had expected to see. "Yes?" Quickly she raked a hand through her tousled hair.

He entered the room, a serious, questioning look on his face. She swallowed and willed her hands to stop trembling. "How are you?" he asked.

"Not so good," she admitted. Her bravado slipped away and tears spilled down her cheeks. Quickly Ethan came to her and held her hands in his, and she sobbed against his shoulder. The fabric of his jacket felt rough on her cheek, but she felt safe and protected.

Haltingly she told him of the diagnosis, adding through her tears, "I don't want them to cut off my leg and finger. I've had them both for sixteen years. I've grown attached to them."

He peered into her swollen eyes. "Of course you are attached to them. But if they have the potential to kill you . . ." He didn't finish the sentence.

"My mother thinks the tests may be wrong. Do you think that's possible?"

"All things are possible."

She clenched her good hand in frustration. "It's not fair, Ethan! Why is God doing this to me?"

"God is not the author of illness," he said patiently.

"Don't defend God to me. If he's God, he can do anything, can't he?"

"Yes—"

"Well, then why did God let this happen to me?" she interrupted.

"We cannot always see God's purposes—"

She waved his answer away. "I don't *care* about purposes. What about my life? I don't want to wear an artificial leg. I don't want people staring at my hand and asking, 'Why's your finger missing?' People will ask, you know. They'll see me as a freak."

"Then that is their problem." Ethan's voice rose to meet the level of hers.

She didn't want pat answers. "It's *my* problem, Ethan. It always will be. How many guys are going to want to date a girl with one leg? Not everybody in the world is a tolerant, kind Amish person, you know."

He recoiled at her sarcasm. "Do you think I don't have questions for God, Leah?"

"What questions could you possibly have?"

His brow was puckered in anger, but his eyes were filled with sadness. "I do not understand why, when there are so many Amish girls, I have to care so much in my heart for an English one."

His words stopped her cold. Fresh tears welled up in her eyes. Then he was holding her face between his large, work-callused palms and kissing her cheeks, her eyelids, her mouth. She thought her heart would leap out of her chest; she thought she would suffocate from sheer delight.

Ethan kissed her, then abruptly stopped and pressed his forehead to hers. She listened to his ragged breathing. "Forgive me," he whispered.

"No," she said.

"I should not—"

She placed her fingers against his lips. "It happened. You can't take it back."

"I did not come here for this."

"Why did you come?" It suddenly occurred to her that he had no reason for being there. And the trip to visit her so close to Christmas probably wasn't approved by his family.

"I dreamed you needed me."

"You dreamed?"

His cheeks colored. "The dream was very real. I felt you were in danger, and that you needed me to be with you."

Until that moment, she hadn't realized how much she did need him. "Will you get in trouble for coming?"

He smiled. "Yes. But I do not care. I *had* to come."

"Does Charity know you're here?"

"She'll figure it out."

"I don't want you to get into trouble because of me."

"I will not leave you."

"Tomorrow, after the test, I'm going home."

"Then I'll stay until you leave."

She felt suddenly shy, awkward. She understood what he was giving her. He was disobeying his community. She should make him leave now, but she didn't have the strength. She needed him. And she wanted him. "Do you have a photo of yourself?" she asked. "I'd like to have it with me when I go home. And I'd like to have it when I come back to the hospital."

He shook his head. "The Amish do not like to be photographed. Preserving our personal image is thought to be prideful and indulgent."

She was disappointed. "But it isn't against your religion, is it?"

"Not strictly." He looked pained and anxious because he couldn't give her what she'd asked for. "I would like a picture of you, Leah."

"I have my school pictures at home. I'll mail one to you." She was glad to be able to give him something tangible of herself to hold on to.

"I will always keep it."

"So now what?" she asked.

"So now we stay together until your test tomorrow."

"Ethan, I'm glad you had the dream. I'm glad you'll be here with me all night."

He hugged her. "I knew I had to see you."

They played video games, they snacked on cookies and apples, they talked until very late. Leah didn't remember falling asleep, yet she awoke with a start and realized that she was in bed in her room. A lamp had been left on, and she peered around the room, looking for Ethan. He wasn't in the room with her. But someone was.

Standing beside her bed was Gabriella.

NINETEEN

"**W**hat do you want?" Leah reached for her call button.

Gabriella looked surprised. "Leah, why are you afraid of me?"

"I—I'm not."

"Yes, you are. I can see it in your eyes. I did not come to harm you."

Leah's fingers touched the call button, but she didn't push it. "Where's Ethan?"

"He went down to the lobby. He'll be back soon."

"Did he tell you that?"

"No. But I know where he's gone."

Leah told herself to call for the night nurse, but she couldn't make herself do it. "You'd better go away before the hospital finds out you're here."

"Is that what you want?"

Suddenly angry, Leah snapped, "Listen, I know you're a fake!"

"A fake?"

"Yes. Molly found out about you visiting me and Rebekah and she's really upset about it. She says she doesn't know who you are or why you're here. But she says you don't belong here."

"Molly said that? But I know Molly well."

"Stop lying!" Leah balled her fist around the covers. "I've got enough trouble without you hanging around. I have cancer, Gabriella. The doctors want to cut off my leg and finger." Leah was shaking with emotion and glaring at the young woman.

Gabriella shook her head. "I know. I didn't come to upset you, Leah. I came to help you."

"Then leave." Leah fought to regain her composure. "You've been nice to me. I don't want to have to turn you in to hospital security."

Gabriella stepped closer to the bed. "I will not see you again, Leah. But I would like you to do me a favor before I go."

"What?"

"There's something in the library for Molly."

"What is it?"

"A gift."

"What kind of a gift?" If Molly didn't know Gabriella, why would Gabriella give her a gift?

"A very special book."

"I don't know . . ."

"She will be very glad to have it."

"How do you know?"

Gabriella smiled. "I just know."

Leah wanted to shout that she was sick of the mysterious smiles and enigmatic conversation. Instead she asked, "Will she really want this book? I don't want to upset her, and she's pretty upset already about you sneaking around the hospital pretending you're a nurse."

"I never said I was a nurse."

"But you acted like one. What else was I supposed to think?"

"I cannot help what you thought. I never pretended to be anybody except myself." Gabriella's voice was soft. She held Leah's gaze, and inexplicably all Leah's fear and anger vanished. She saw a beautiful woman with gentle brown eyes. "You have many questions," Gabriella said.

"Yes," Leah answered, her voice barely a whisper.

"It will take a lifetime to answer them." Gabriella reached out to Leah. "I have a gift for you too, Leah."

"What?" Gabriella took Leah's hands in hers and placed them on Leah's wrapped knee. Then she tenderly covered Leah's hands with her own. Warmth from their combined touches spread through her sore knee.

"Do you want to be well?"

"Of course."

"Then *believe*."

"Believe what?"

"Believe in the power and goodness of God."

"I—I believe . . ." Leah stared into Gabriella's eyes, and suddenly she *did* believe. She believed in a power higher and stronger than what could be seen or explained. She closed her eyes, and a feeling of peace enveloped her. When she opened her eyes, she was alone, still clutching her knee. All she saw was the darkened corners of her room and the lamp glowing on the table. Nothing remained of Gabriella.

* * *

Leah told Ethan everything, but he could make no sense of it either. "Perhaps you fell asleep and dreamed this," he suggested. "How does your leg feel?"

She rotated it. "I'm not sure. About the same, I guess."

"Did she frighten you?"

"A little. She's strange. And after what Molly said about—" She interrupted herself. "Ethan! Help me to the library."

"Why?"

"Gabriella said there was a book in the library that would mean a lot to Molly."

"What book?"

"I don't know, but I need to find it."

He helped her with her crutches and walked with her as she hobbled down the dimly lit hall. In the library, Leah peered around at the shelves.

"How will you know which is the right book?" Ethan said.

Leah didn't know what drew her to the right side of the room, to the third shelf, halfway over. But that was where she instinctively went. She leaned against the bookcase, handed one crutch to Ethan and gingerly tugged a small book off the shelf. The book was worn, bound in green leather, and fastened tightly with an old-fashioned clasp lock. The lock wouldn't budge. "This is it."

"How do you know?"

"I just know."

Ethan swept his hand over her hair. She looked into his eyes and forgot about the book, forgot about everything except his nearness. "You are beautiful, Leah. And I know that you will be all right."

Her heart pounded crazily. "What makes you say that?"

"Because it is Christmas." His smile almost lit the room. "And because I do not lie."

Leah was taken down to X ray first thing in the morning. She introduced her mother to Ethan as "my guardian angel," and when he looked startled, she patted his hand and said, "It's just a figure of speech."

She endured the radioactive injection, sat and talked to Ethan and her mother while it was absorbed into her bones, and lay perfectly still on the table for the scanning camera. Then she returned to her room and started to pack. She was almost finished when the X-ray department sent for her a second time.

Again she went down to X ray, where a very agitated technician said she had to repeat the procedure.

"Why again?" her mother demanded. "Can't you get it right?"

"Look, lady, I know how to do my job, but whatever her doctor's looking for didn't show up clear enough, so I have to do it again."

Leah glanced at Ethan, who shrugged and squeezed her hand.

Much later, as she was leaving the floor to go home—in a wheelchair, as all patients were required to do—Molly hurried up to her. "I'm so glad I caught you. I wanted to say goodbye and let you know I'll be here after the holidays when you come back." She saw Ethan and looked surprised.

"I came to keep her company," he explained.

Leah remembered the book and reached into her bag. "I have something for you. Actually, it's from Gabriella."

"She came to see you?" Molly looked alarmed.

"Don't be worried. She won't be back." Leah handed Molly the book. "She wanted you to have this."

Molly took it, then gasped. All the color

drained from her face. "Where did she get this?"

"What is it? What's wrong?" Seeing Molly's reaction made Leah's heart skip.

"It's my sister's diary. It's been missing for all these years. We knew Emily kept it. I saw her writing in it, but after she died, we couldn't find it anywhere." Molly hugged the book to herself as tears streamed down her face.

"Gabriella told me it was in the library, and that's exactly where Ethan and I found it."

"How can that be? That library's been revamped and restocked many times over the years. Someone would have found it before now."

"I don't know how," Leah said, equally baffled. "But that's where we found it. Just like Gabriella said we would. It's locked."

"I have the key. I've kept it all these years." Molly wiped her eyes. "Oh, Leah, what a wonderful present for my parents. We're supposed to go there for Christmas dinner. I'll take it with me and we'll read it together." She looked at Leah. "Thank you. And thank this Gabriella when you see her."

"She told me that I won't see her again," Leah said. "And I believe her."

The elevator door slid open. "Let's blow this place," Leah's mother said.

In the lobby, they waited for Leah's mother to drive the car to the front door. Outside, snow was falling. Leah saw a gray van off to one side. Ethan touched Leah's cheek. "My ride to Nappanee is waiting for me. I must go."

Leah clung to his hand, not wanting him to leave her. "Ethan, I want you to know how much it mattered to me to have you come stay with me."

"I wanted to stay with you."

"I don't want you to be in trouble because of it."

"I cannot change what I have done." He squared his jaw. "You should not worry about me."

"I'll write you. Charity and Rebekah, too."

He grinned and stroked her hair. "We'll wait for your letter."

"Please tell them Merry Christmas, and that it helped knowing they were praying for me."

"So are you no longer angry with God?"

She sighed. "I guess not. I need his help, don't I?"

He bent and kissed her forehead. "Merry Christmas, English."

"Merry Christmas," she whispered. She watched him step out into the snow, his dark coat, pants and broad-brimmed hat stark against the white snow. She pressed her hand to her mouth and felt the lingering warmth of his touch. She watched him disappear into the van, and she hoped with all her heart that angels would watch over him forever.

TWENTY

January 30

Dear Charity,

Thanks for your letter. I *love* hearing from you. I'm mailing you two letters in this envelope, one for you and Rebekah, the other for Ethan. Could you please give it to him?

Since you asked for my news, I'll give it to you in detail. Where to begin? . . . I went back to the hospital right after New Year's Day and Mom, Neil and I met with Dr. Thomas and two of his colleagues. I wish you could have been there. It's hard to write down what happened, but I'll try.

Dr. Thomas hung four sets of my X rays on his light board, which included a series he'd had done that very morning. The first few sets of X rays showed big dark spots where cancer had eaten away my bone. But on the newest set of X rays the spots were smaller! He explained that the X rays were showing that the cancer wasn't nearly as advanced as they originally thought. So I endured another biopsy which showed that while there were still some questionable cells, the doctors felt that after a round of chemotherapy, I'll eventually be all right. In other words, NO amputation! What a relief!

Mom went ballistic (which means crazy-angry). She shouted, "What if you'd cut off Leah's leg and then found you'd made a mistake? Then what would you say?" Dr. Thomas insisted he hadn't made a mistake. He assured us his diagnosis had been correct. He explained that sometimes X rays can look different from each other, but he did agree that he was mystified by the shrinking spots. He showed us some pretty interesting stories in a medical book about patients who go into "spontaneous remission" with absolutely no help from medical science. He admitted that there really *are* some weird unexplained healings. I mean people who were at death's door—much worse off than me—and then their sicknesses mysteriously vanished over time. That's when Dr. Thomas recommended chemo. He said it was the smart, responsible thing to do. I'm not crazy about taking it (I'll probably lose my hair and be sick), but I guess it's best not to take a chance that I'm not having a "spontaneous remission."

Neil was real quiet through the whole discussion. But right after Dr. Thomas finished with his explanations, Neil says, " 'Spontaneous remissions'—in my day we called them miracles." It made me laugh, and, of course, think of you and Rebekah. It also made everybody in the room relax a little.

Anyway Dr. Thomas agreed that there were some things science couldn't explain. Whether we call it a spontaneous remission or a miracle doesn't matter to me. All I know is that I still have my leg. And in spite of having to go through chemo, I have a good feeling about this, Charity. You might even say I have faith. Maybe your prayers for me helped after all.

Which brings me to the part Gabriella may have played in all of this. Only Rebekah and I ever saw her. But she *did* exist. Emily's diary is proof enough for me. Molly can't understand how it could have been in the library all these years and nobody ever found it. It's a real mystery, and only Gabriella knows the answer.

Speaking of books, did I mention that I got my own Bible for Christmas? I've been doing a lot of reading in it, especially about angels. I keep thinking of all the things you told me about them the night we decorated the Christmas tree, and so-o-o, I'm going to tell you something that may make you think I've gone nuts. Charity, I think that Gabriella might be an angel. That would explain so many things about her. The way she seemed to appear and disappear. The way I felt so peaceful the last night I saw her. She may even be responsible for the craziness with my X rays! I honestly can't find another way to explain the things that have happened.

But you're smarter about these things, what do you think?

Anyway, I *do* know that you and Rebekah and Ethan are angels too. *Earth* angels who came into my life when I needed a miracle! Thanks for your friendship. Please keep writing and tell Rebekah that if she ever sees Gabriella again, she should throw a net over her. I have a hundred questions I want to ask her.

Leah

Dear Reader,

Would you do me a favor? Would you lend this book to a friend? I get so many letters from young people saying they love to share my books with their friends, and I like knowing that my stories are being read by as many people as possible—people like the reader who wrote, "I cry when I read your books, but I love them. They make me realize that life isn't always 'happily ever after.'"

If you enjoyed this story, why not share your experience with a friend by passing this book along? My publishers think this request is important enough to leave a blank page where you can write a private note to your friend when you pass along the book. They think others will feel inspired when they read about people facing life-and-death experiences with courage and hope. Maybe you can tell your friend why you like this book and why you think she should read it. And if you just can't stand to part with your copy, you can tear out the book list (which is on the other side of the blank page) to give to a friend.

I love writing books. I love knowing that kids enjoy reading my books. And I love knowing they're sharing my books with their friends. Thank you for your loyalty. And keep reading!

Best wishes,

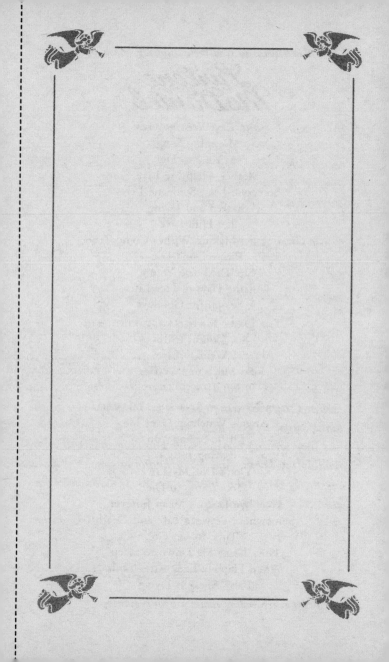